I & I

I & I

Mark A. Mills

2006

I & I

CONTENTS

Poetry

ENTER THE GREAT HOUSE

For the goddess Maat: the ancient Egyptian goddess of truth. She also represents justice, law, morality and order. Belief in Maat was the foundation for Egyptian spirituality. It was the duty of the pharaoh to exemplify and uphold the concept of Maat. Moreover, when a person died, the person's heart was placed on the dual scales of justice. The heart, not the brain, was placed on the scale because the Egyptians believed that one's key decisions were made in the heart. On the other scale was a feather, which symbolized Maat, or truth. If the heart and the feather did not balance, the deceased was thrown into a burning pit with demons and starving alligators with snapping jaws.

A note on the cover: The ancient Egyptian Eyes of Horus (or Eyes of Ra) are known as *udjat* ("Whole"). They are a powerful symbol of protection, and thought to confer wisdom, health and prosperity. While Ra (or Amen-Ra) is the Supreme Being, Horus is the fourth-most critical Egyptian religious figure. Horus, symbolized also by the bird of prey, the fierce falcon, represents the avenging son of Osiris. Horus succeeded his father to become the second pharaoh. His right eye is the sun and his left eye is the moon. His mother was Isis. His father was Osiris, who was murdered by his brother, Set. Horus battled Set to avenge his father's death, winning the battle but losing an eye in the process. The eye was restored by the magic of Thot, the god of wisdom and writing. The Eye of Horus symbol was used in funerary rites, per the Egyptian *Book of Coming Forth by Day* (aka *the Book of the Dead*) as a means of protection. It was also used to represent fractions, based on repeated division by two.

The ancient Egyptian cross, the ankh, represents eternal life, fertility, and the fusion of male and female energy. If the heart of the deceased was as light as Maat's feather (which symbolized truth; the scales would be balanced and it would mean that the deceased was able to say that she did not violate the 42 negative confessions, which are the precursor to the 10 commandments), the ankh would then be placed to her lips to give her "The Breath of Life," so that she could chill with the lord of the underworld, Osiris, in the heavenly afterlife, a beautiful place with lush green fields, where her soul could live for eternity.

By having symbols of Horus and Ra on either side of the ankh, the cover symbolizes two main tenets of ancient Egyptian spirituality: regeneration—the avenging son shall always rise. And balance. The right eye reflects masculine solar energy while the left eye represents feminine lunar energy. Combined, they represent both the transcendent power of Horus and the comprehensive ("udjat") universe, a concept similar to the Taosit yin-yang concept.

Lastly, the Eye of Providence symbol found above the pyramid on American currency, the Rx pharmaceutical symbol and the Masonic all-seeing eye originate from the Eye of Horus.

"I and I a conqueror! You no see dem a come? I and I a conqueror!"
The lyrics of the bi-racial Bob Nesta Marley refer to he and his
God
or "Him and him people dem, you know, I?"

"Even if they shoot me down!/
There'll be another bigga nigga!/
from the Underground!"

From "I Don't Give a Fuck," The *2pacalypse Now* album

Tupac Amaru Shakur
aka Makavelli the Don
aka Shinning Serpent

For Ra

ANCIENT EGYPTIAN SPIRITUALITY

***

ANCIENT EGYPTIAN SPIRITUALITY

0...Amen

Value 0: Amen: To remain peaceful in the face of all disruptions.

Symbol: The symbol of Amen is seven hieroglyphic symbols, one of which is the symbol of Maat/truth, the feather. Amen is the highest point on the Tree of Life, 0; and the most important of all the Tree of Life values. Amen is defined as "concealed," as the Supreme Being is concealed, unseen or hidden. Zero is the potential of all things. Amen (or Amun or Ra) is the omnipresent Supreme Being and again, believed to be without form, hidden. To be clear, the Egyptians believed in monotheism. Ra was and is thee God. Represented by a solar disk, He is the Almighty, the hidden one, the creator of all mankind and all realms, the invisible God who is omnipresent. His living equal and incarnation was the pharaoh/the great house.

Ancient Egyptian Spirituality is Maat: Belief in truth (speak it from your heart, let it cling to your lips), justice (be fair to all in your actions) and harmony (righteousness and generosity in community); and the belief in the interdependence of all things. For example: the way man needs woman and the way woman complements and completes man, the way that we depend on the earth to feed and nourish us, the way that the earth depends on us not to abuse it and the way that we depend on our bodies and our bodies depend on us.

The goal of Ancient Egyptian Spirituality: To awaken the divinity within us so that we can be an expression of the Supreme Being's love, and achieve the highest level of both spirituality and inner peace: Amen.

How to achieve the goal: Mediation through the Tree of Life meditation system and actions that represent the Tree of Life's values, the first of which is Amen.

The Tree of Life Mediation System consists of 11 Values:
0. Amen
1. Ausar,
2. Tehuti
3. Seker
4. Maat
5. Herukhuti
6. Heru
7. Het-Heru
8. Sebek
9. Auset
10. Geb

For more on the Tree of Life, see Ra Un Nefer Amen's *Tree of Life Mediation System,* and the *Metu Neter (Words of God) Volumes 1 and 2.*

The ancient Egyptians believed in monotheism. Their name for the Supreme Being was Amen or Ra (although there are other names for God, these are the two most widely used, e.g., sometimes "Amen" is called "Amun" and "Ra" is called "Re"). The other names of gods and goddesses you hear and read about are symbols of the Supreme Being or what we would consider today as saints. When the first pharaoh of Egypt united the north and south, one region called the Supreme Being Amen, and the other called it Ra. To show his respect for the land and the people he conquered, he combined the two and called the Supreme being Amen-Ra, thereby facilitating peace throughout the land then known as Kamit, "the land of the blacks." Does the face of Sphinx look like African? Today the word "Amen" can be found in various usages, most notably in the Catholic church. In Italian, "re" means "king."

ANCIENT EGYPTIAN SPIRTUALITY

I...Ausar

Value I: Ausar/Osiris: To filter all things through Ra (the name of the Supreme Being, and it dwells inside each human).

Symbol: The pharaoh Ausar/Osiris wearing the tall crown with the bulbous top and holding the crook and the flail, the symbols of sovereignty.

When you go to the awe-inspiring Temple of Amun at Karnak, in romantic Luxor, Egypt, you will see his statue. He looks like a young cat on '2-5 in Harlem.

The Egyptians used the word Ra to describe the indwelling God because they believed Ra gave them life, like the sun gives life to all things. Ausar is symbolized as a pharaoh holding the crook and the flail, and wearing the tall tapering white crown of Upper Egypt, the region that unified Upper and Lower Egypt. Ausar is sometimes also depicted as a mummified body, which symbolizes unshakeable inner peace and the ability to be uncorrupted by sensual and emotional temptations. It was believed that Ausar was, like Ra, the indwelling divinity in all things and the source of peace and prosperity in the world. This was believed because it was thought that Ra created Ausar, and as such Ausar/Osiris was God's living embodiment on Earth. Of divine birth, Ausar/Osiris was believed to be God's representative on

Earth. In this first pharaoh, man had been made into God's image. And for this reason, each subsequent pharaoh was thought to be of divine birth, which is why all subsequent pharaohs had to be male.* For reasons to be explained later, Ausar would also come to be known also as Osiris, lord of the dead/lord of those coming forth by day and lord of the underworld (wherein in one makes the passage from death to life, death to eternal life or death to damnation).

Order of dieties, just in case you're getting confused:
0. Ra (aka Re, Amun, Amen, Amun-Re, Amun-Ra)
1. Osiris (aka Ausar)
2. Isis (aka Auset)
3. Horus (aka Heru)

So now, imagine a triangle: on top you have Ra, at the bottom right you have Ausar/Osiris and on the left you Auset/Isis and in the center you have the son, Horus/Heru.

A common daily Egyptian prayer:
Thou sole and only One!
Thou Sun God who hath none other like Him!
Protector of millions, savior of hundreds of thousands
Who shieldeth him who calleth upon Him
Thou Lord of On
Punish me not for my many sins
I am one ignorant of my own body!
Each day I follow after my own dictates as
The ox after his own fodder!
Come to me, O Ra!
That thou mayest guide me!

A common theme throughout Egyptian spirituality is showing remorse for violating the values of the Tree of Life. To disobey its values was to violate Amen, Maat (truth, which they held sacred) and oneself; this remorse is also known as the sorrows of Ausar.

*A note about sexism in ancient Egyptian society: Women could hold the highest positions and were respected as equals, except when it came to being pharaoh. Only men could become pharaohs, e.g., Cleopatra ruled Egypt but was not a pharaoh. But one queen dared to become pharaoh. As mentioned earlier, because the first pharaoh was male and created in God's image, it was believed that all pharaohs had to be male or it was an act against God.

ANCIENT EGYPTIAN SPIRITUALITY

2...Tehuti

Value 2: Tehuti: To use words of power to overcome all obstacles.

Symbol: The ibis-headed man wearing a double-plumed crown and holding a scroll and a writing instrument.

These words of power are chants, as well as wise words that come to the initiate of Egyptian spirituality intuitively when needed. Tehuti is the writer, or what was called the scribe. This revered position knew all the words of power and could, depending on the depth of his or her faith in Maat and success in the wisdom system/Tree of Life rituals of the Egyptian priesthood, perform what is today called magic, or what the Egyptians then called science.

There was no difference in using the skill set of the priesthood to manipulate electromagnetic forces to move three-ton pyramid blocks or to part a river to find a dropped earring. Such was the power of the most accomplished scribes-turned-priests-turned professionals. Scribes, who later became priests, could continue their long and arduous study by going into the professions, e.g., higher levels of the clergy, law, architecture, mathematics (the Egyptians invented quadractic equations, the mathematical foundation of science), economics, astronomy, medicine, politics (some scribes would rise to become secretary of state, also know as the vizier, of the pharaoh). Some scribes would rise to become pharaoh.

The vizier was expected to always have the right answer. He was ambassador, wartime counselor, consoling priest to the queen who had lost a son in battle, and on rare occasion, he was called upon to be an assassin. The symbol of the scribe is the god of writing, Thot, who is depicted as an ibis-headed man holding a writing palette. Thot was also the god of the moon, wisdom and learning. He was often shown in the underworld at the "weighing of the heart ceremony." Thot recorded the verdict of the Maat, as the scales remained even or tipped to one side. The Egyptians used the image of the ibis because when the ibis dipped his head into the water for prey, he did not miss.

So, picture if you will, your death, your soul leaving your body, traveling on a solar ray into the heavens into a dark underworld. You are met by giant black gates, and demons, and out of nowhere comes a jackal-headed man to guide you, Anubis. He takes you by the hand, through the towering gates that are so ominous they make you gulp. He guides you safely past the demons, until you reach the graceful goddess Maat, who awaits you with her scales, upon which is your heart and her feather. You are asked the 42 negative confessions questions: 42 questions that are the precursors to the 10 commandments. You have to say "no" to each confession—and if you lie, the scale with your heart will tip, revealing your lie. The questions continue for what seem like an eternity. Images of your actions play out like a movie, as Maat, Thot and you watch your actions, or re-watch your actions. Did you not do this or did you not do that, e.g., Did you kill? Did you commit adultery? Standing next to you as you speak, copiously recording your words, is the ibis-headed man, Thot. Is the scale moving, or is it even? Are you sweating or are you cool? Is your heart at peace? The goddess Maat requests your confession.

This is how you maintain an ordered civilzed culture for over 7,000 years. The ancient Egyptians believed strongly that there will be a pointy reckoning, a judgment day.

Magic/Science: Modern Egyptologists can theorize how the three-ton blocks were moved to create the pyramids, but can they tell you how they were cut? A stone's throw away from the first pyramid, the step pyramid, is an underground structure. The passage way leading down is narrow and it looks like poured concrete. How did they do that? The ancient Egyptians had a saying: It is not a matter of building high, but building deep. The ingenious cantilevered ceiling of the red pyramid, how was that built?

The 7 Principles of Maat, which the Egyptians attempted to follow daily:
   Justice: be fair to all in your actions
   Order: internal discipline and development
   Balance: the right measure in all good things
   Harmony: righteousness and generosity in community
   Propriety: loyalty and service to those respected
   Reciprocity: do for another, so that he or she may also do
   Truth: speak it from your heart, let it cling to you lips

Isis/Auset: The queen mother, or original virgin Mary, has many titles, including lady of the house of fire, the beautiful goddess, the lady of words of power. She is well known for her facility with words of power. She pronounced them in such a way that the individuals or things to which they were addressed were compelled to do as she wished. The Egyptians believed that words of power must be uttered in a certain tone of voice, and at a certain pace and pitch, and at a certain time of the day or night, with appropriate gestures or ceremonies to produce the intended result. In the Hymn to her husband Ausar/Osiris, it is dramatized that Isis used her skill in words of power to restore her husband to life, and obtained from him an heir: Horus, the anointed savior. She obtained these words from Thoth, the "lord of divine words."

Isis is the most powerful of all goddesses. Goddess of funeral rites, she is also known as the giver of life because she gave birth to Horus. She is associated with the bringing of new soil, crops and food to people who worship her. Isis is usually depicted as a woman with the hieroglyph for the word "throne" on her head. She is often shown in Egyptian art as mourning her husband Osiris or nursing her son Horus. The latter image is the precursor to the Madonna and child paintings of Europe. She is also the model for the Virgin Mary paintings. The earliest versions of both types of paintings feature black women and have been found in the Catholic churches of Europe. Look at a Madonna and child painting and then look at a wall painting (or sculpture) of Isis nursing Horus.

ANCIENT EGYPTIAN SPIRITUALITY

3...Seker

Seker: To use my ab (heart), my ba (my soul, which flies to heaven), my will, my ka (the double of my soul that stays earth bound and embodies statues of me; ka alos means "conscience"), my Ra (the life force within me), and my ability to ignore—to use all of these to achieve all objectives.

Symbol: The falcon-headed man seated upon a throne holding the crook, the flail, and the uas scepter: all powerful symbols of the right to govern.

The Egyptians would use their ability to ignore to help them become more moral by ignoring lustful impulses, thereby utilizing the value of Amen (to remain peaceful in the face of all disruptions), while facilitating the primary goal of achieving unshakeable inner peace: to become God-like on Earth. They strived to achieve happiness and joy by seeking the highest possible spiritual cultivation. They practiced how to will themselves to be joyful in the face of any situation or setback, achieving what the Indians later called Nirvana.

The Ancient Egyptians' View of How the World was Created: In sum, they believed that when the world was born, there was only primordial water and darkness. A lotus blossom emerged from the depths. Ra, the sun, rose from this white and gold blossom. Ra created four children: males Shu (air) and Geb (earth) and females Tefnut (moisture) and Nut (sky). The first divine couple of Geb and Nut produced two sons, Set (as in "set it off" or "setback") and Osiris, as well as two daughters, Isis and Nephthys. Osiris succeeded Ra as pharaoh of the Earth, and was aided by Isis. However, his jealous and envious brother despised him and ultimately killed him. Isis found Osiris's dead body and using magic spells, she became pregnant with Horus through immaculate conception. Osiris was resurrected (this is the first known resurrection of the Creator's son). Osiris was resurrected as god of the underworld, the land the dead must pass through at night before going on to the Egyptian equivalents of heaven or hell. When Osiris's son Horus grew into manhood, he avenged his father by defeating Set. Horus became pharaoh of the Earth.

In Ra you have the unseen almighty God. In Osiris you have God on Earth and the first resurrection story. In Horus you have the anointed savior come to life through the first immaculate conception story. In Isis, you have Mary, mother of God's representative on earth, mother to Horus through immaculate conception, and the first "Madonna and Child."

The Egyptian Holy Trinity: Osiris (God's representative as Pharaoh, Jesus as pharaoh; Jesus resurrected), Isis (the virgin Mary) and Horus (God's only begotten son, Jesus reborn). Osiris is also known as Ausar. He represents the dead, especially a deceased pharaoh. At each hour of the night, the dead must go through a different section of the underworld. They enter each section through a gate and are met by different demons. They are guided by the god of embalming, the Jackal headed-Anubis, who helped Isis mummify Osiris/Ausar.

Horus is symbolized as a falcon or a falcon-headed man because of the falcon's majestic and imperious form, its ability to soar among the heavens with beauty and grace, and its skill in destroying its prey. Horus is seen as the divine symbol of kingship and as a protector of both the pharaoh and Kamit/Egypt.

ANCIENT EGYPTIAN SPIRITUALITY

4...Maat

Maat: to live truth, justice and harmony. To realize the interdependence of all things.

Symbol: A woman with a feather in her hair holding the scales of justice.

"Maat" also means "what is right." It is symbolized by the goddess who wears a feather in her hair. The feather epitomizes the lightness of truth and is balanced against the heart of a person who died before they pass into the afterlife. If the heart remains as light as the feather, the person transcends into the heavenly afterlife with the god of the afterlife, Osiris.

The question for Egyptians at the end of each day was: Did I live truthfully? Did I obey the divine laws of Maat? If they did not, they showed great remorse and struggled to do better the next day. Using the value system listed on the first spirituality page, they were able to see where they were going wrong. They realized that to cultivate the strength required to live by the divine laws they would have to develop their indwelling life-force—the solar energy within them—their Ra/Ausar/Osiris—by eating healthy (no pork), exercising (yoga or some form of strength training and regular cardio) and moderately engaging in sensual pleasures. Great strength is required to be incorruptible. Great strength is required to be God-like.

ANCIENT EGYPTIAN SPIRITUALITY

5... Herukhuti

Herukhuti: To be able to defend yourself where there seems to be no means to do so.

Symbol: The falcon-headed man holding a spear and a dagger. As pharaoh Tutankhamen might say, "Welcome to my town, motherfuckers!" This value governs the military.

This principle is the birthplace of karma and the golden rule. Very personally, it is first and foremost, to control one's being, as we are defined by the choices we make. "Pharaoh" means "the great house." Each individual had to measure herself or himself against the spiritual and moral example set by the pharaoh, the beacon of divine law. They had to ask themselves if they were being fair and honest, first of all, with themselves.

Pharaoh Hatshepsut: What exemplifies a legend most? Composure. Her ability to hold her head when all about her were losing theirs and blaming it on her? Cool as a breeze off the Nile in spring, the first woman pharaoh of Kamit was known for her calm under pressure. Her son Thutmose III became pharaoh at a very young age and Hatshepsut was named regent. Some years later, roughly 1473 B.C., after leading Kamit to peace and prosperity as regent, she donned the royal male ceremonial regalia and had the high priests perform the secret and sacred rights to swear her in as pharaoh, the living embodiment of God, the ruler of divine birth, God made in human form. Fifteen or 20 years, and many triumphs later, her son decided this God's reign was over. He wanted what was his by divine law: "The pharaoh is, was, and always will be a male! Let her be slain and let her names be stricken from every stone and papyrus throughout Kamit! Pharaoh has spoken!"

Her coronation name: Maatkara, the living homage to God and truth, was to be erased. Thutmose III wanted what was stolen from him. His mother, Hatshepsut, soon disappeared and her name chiseled out of every monument in the land. She had done what her grandfather could not do, she had done what her father could not do—she had defeated the alien invaders who had taken over regions of the land and threatened to takeover the entire country. This woman who brought genius and practicality to all things she touched defeated the dreaded Hyskos. It did not matter. She was a woman. And she was gone.

ANCIENT EGYPTIAN SPIRITUALITY

6...Heru

Heru: To control all emotional and sensual desires. "Heru" (or "Horus") means "hero." Herus is man's will and governs all positions of leadership.

Symbol: The falcon-headed man wearing the double crown of Upper and Lower Kamit/Egypt. He holds two scepters, one being the shekem scepter (symbol of mighty power of the underworld, i.e., Osiris).

ANCIENT EGYPTIAN SPIRITUALITY

7...Het-heru

Het-heru: To awaken and direct all energies using my imagination.

Symbol: A woman smelling a lotus flower.

"Het-Heru" means the house of the hero, where the house is one's mind, body and soul. For example, imagine a scenario where you are overcoming one of your personal challenges, breathe deeply 10 times, and then meditate on overcoming the challenge. You are awakening and directing all energies using your imagination: by awakening your unconscious you are empowering your imagination. It's akin to the visualizing-success technique used by basketball great Michael Jordan.

Enter the Great House: Enter "the great house," means enter "the pharaoh": Master of self. Master of the God within.

What it means to be hard: In Bed-Stuy, Brooklyn, guys always talk about being a hard rock, being hard. What does it mean to be the rock? For the Egyptians, it meant being comprehensive in purpose: This is what I'm about. You can check it, because I represent it each day, every day, in thought and action. I walk it—I talk it—I am it. I breathe it. There is no weakness in my game. There is no crack in my façade. I am the rock. The duality between my conscious and unconscious is joined and made whole by my indwelling God. You will not find me saying one thing (my conscious will) and doing another (my stronger unconscious will). You will not find me corrupted. The Sphinx in Giza best represents this notion of the hard rock. The ultimate strong silent type. Head of man (the ability to reason). Breast of a woman (the ability to be compassionate). The body of lion (the ability to destroy all prey as king of the beasts). Unshakeable. Incorruptible. Calm in the face of all disruptions (value number zero, Amen. Zero, the potential of all things).

The Sphinx is the epitome of transformation—from life to death to life, from man to beast, from woman to free will, from warrior to compassionate ruler (of the great house) and back again—least of which is the ability to fly, ascending to the heavens in much the same way that the pyramid symbolizes the fire of creativity, a flame that licks the heavens.

This same concept is found in the mythic phoenix—regeneration, coming forth anew. It is you! Your ability to transform who you are, the way you are constantly changing, in body, in mind, in spirit, whether you acknowledge it or not, coming closer to death, coming closer to life, constantly transforming from one form into another.

But what lives on? The spirit never dies. It no longer returns to Earth after becoming the rock. Then it is Amen and resides with Osiris in the heavenly afterlife. In each royal pyramid, there is a narrow window/portal that allowed the sun's ray to enter on a certain day and beam down to the coffin of the deceased ruler. And on this day, the pharaoh's soul/ba would ascend to the heavens on a ray of sunlight, rising like a flame to the heavens and the afterlife.

ANCIENT EGYPTIAN SPIRITUALITY

8...Sebek

Sebek: To awaken and direct all energies using my intellect.

Symbol: The jackal-headed man Anpu/Anubis with his arms crossed. Sometimes he is symbolized as a crocodile, a baboon or a dog.

With Het-heru, the Egyptians used images, with Sebek they used words. Sebek means the planet Mercury, aka the messenger. It uses a process similar to the one described in value number 7 to articulate nonverbal messages that are in harmony with one's indwelling intelligence. This allowed the Egyptians to communicate effectively about complex matters related to the heart and mind. The symbol for Sebek is Anubis, the jackal-headed man, who leads the dead through the underworld (one's subconscious).

ANCIENT EGYPTIAN SPIRITUALITY

9...Auset

Auset: To have pre-knowledge of all events by programming my subconscious.

Symbol: Auset nursing Horus/Madonna and Child.

This corresponds to the Egyptians' will to achieve a distinct goal by using the preceding two processes, which unite the will to the indwelling solar-force, or chi, by using meditation as a conduit to the unconscious. Women have a higher ability to utilize meditation to achieve values 7-9. But all can achieve the highest, most critical values: 0-3. Again we see the ancient Egyptians using mental power to change reality, changing the vibration of the conscious and unconscious mind to effect material change.

ANCIENT EGYPTIAN SPIRITUALITY

10...Geb

Geb: To have the physical strength to carry out Ra's will.

This means regular cardio (keeping the heart strong), crunches or core strength (the abs are the most important area, as they support the frame of the house and one's back), a healthy diet (high in fruit, low in meat, as this supplies natural energy; eating a lot of superfoods, such as broccoli) and moderate sensual pleasures (balance: the right measure in all good things).

Obelisks/"Tejen": Made of one solid piece of stone in the shape of a sun beam, these structures—at least 30-meters high—symbolize the solar ray on which the pharaoh's spirit ascends to heaven. Thus, they symbolize both the solar power of regeneration and Ra. From the top down the obelisk represents (mathematically) a sun-beam; from the bottom up, it represents a phallic symbol of Ra. An obelisk broadcasts or radiates its text/image both to the light above consciousness, and to the subconscious sexuality. The obelisk's substance is the essence of earth (stone). But it is earth as it reunites with heaven, embodying myths of solar ascension and of the penetrating spirit of light. Its uprightness and pyramid shape point to the celestial impulse. The quadrangle base of the obelisk ends in a pyramidal, typically capped with gold, which the Egyptians believed to be "the flesh of the gods." Obelisks, or Tejen, in ancient Egyptian, were also synonymous with protection or defense. They had the function of perforating the clouds and dispersing negative forces in the form of visible or invisible storms. Usually two obelisks were placed outside the temple as stone symbols of the Supreme Being's almighty power. There are only approximately 30 of these monoliths remaining on Earth. Romans, obsessed with them, appropriated 13 to Italy (placing many outside churches). One is in Central Park in New York City. One is in London looking out over the River Thames (a potent combination of life's cardinal elements—fire and water—or what the Taoists call yin and yang energies, which in combination achieve harmonious balance). Approximately five tejen remain in the land of the pharaohs.

It is believed by some that America's inauthentic obelisk, the Washington Monument in the U.S. capital, was built as a form of worship to Ra by America's early leaders, many of whom were freemasons, a group which uses obelisks in its secret rituals and rites of passage.

It's interesting to note that the image of Solar Horus: the falcon with it's wings spread and holding lotuses (symbols of regeneration) in its talons, is very similar to the image of the American eagle mascot found on the one dollar bill; the American eagle is on the right and on the left is the symbol of the pyramid with the all-seeing eye. For the pharaohs, the Solar Horus was the king's protector and represented his divine authority.

PROSE

✹✹✹

PROSE

0…The Longest Mile

A 12-year-old girl walked for a day from "the bush"/the rural areas of Kingston, Jamaica, where she lived with her mother and three half-sisters. The girl walked and walked until she got to City Hall. She stared at the building's gold dome against the velvety twilight, wondering—*responsibility, dignity, class, strength, respect*—what did they mean outside of the corporal-punishment classroom? What did they mean in *real life*? Were they all an illusion? Was everything just bullshit. *Power?*

Her shoulders begged to slump from exhaustion, but she wouldn't let them. She cursed herself as weak. She spied benches in the park across the street and thought for an instant about a momentary respite, but turned her head sharply, as if disgusted with herself for even having the thought. She trooped on to her final destination on sore soles. Nearing her destination, she walked into a gas station bathroom to freshen up. She looked in the mirror at the luggage under her eyes and hated being born black. *Bastard. A black bastard. That's what you are! Lucky for you that you're half pretty and light, because if you weren't, then you'd really be in trouble, bitch! Then nobody would want you! You bastard! She spat in the mirror!*

She proceeded into the center of Kingston, unnerved by the crowded streets and congested traffic, its rank smell of diesel fuel mixing with dust and open-air food markets. She ignored the advances of boys on loud motor scooters aggressively riding up alongside her and revving their motors to get her attention.

She looked up at the garish yellow neon sign outside of an establishment: *Carlton's.*

The former interim mayor of Kingston owned that bar. She walked out of the dusk and into the dark bar. It smelled faintly of stale beer. A little old bald man—98 pounds wet—knelt on the wooden floor, briskly unpacking cases of beer from cardboard boxes, ripping open the boxes with a vengeance. He was tan, wiry and late. He thought about how timing was everything. He ran the month's profits through his calculator-like mind. He didn't hear the door open or the cat-like softness of her steps. He looked up at her dirty bare feet and then at her face. He was slightly surprised. She looked into in his Chinese eyes and saw her own. The same shape. The same color. The same bags, only hers were just forming. She felt a pang of regret at the sight of him. *Father...Finally.* What should she do? He did not know her but knew well the look she shot him. Hate and love battling in one small body. Hate would win, so fuck it. Neither father nor daughter was much for small talk.

I need money.

You must be mad gal! Me not married to you mada! You mada was just a one-night stand! You no mean *a ting* to me! Gwan!

He brushed her away with his hand. She did not move. Any love she might have felt for him died in the next instant. She stepped closer.

The multibusiness owner with numerous illegitimate children all over Jamaica waved her away again—*Me say Gwan!* He resumed unpacking, but with more severity. She didn't move. The ripping cardboard echoed in the dank bar, whose linoleum floors faintly smelled of ammonia. The girl fought back tears. Slowly, she replaced them with fury. *Class.* She looked down at him, and the bottles, attempting to resist the slow seduction of violence.

She walked out of the bar looking straight ahead and into the pedestrian-packed streets. Large speakers on the streets blared quick tempo dancehall music now, each store's speakers competed with the next. All the clubs and bars on Kingston's main drag were getting ready for another "hot hot!" Saturday night. *Hot like love!*

She recorded the day in her memory. She stopped an old woman returning from Church and asked her the time. She wanted to be able to look back on this day and the exact time. *She looked at the woman's fine church dress, powder blue with lots of sequins, as the woman smiled warmly and turned to go. She felt that it was a sign from God. She hated church and God. She heard a voice say, "You are loved. I am inside you. You are me and I am you. Have faith in me. Come closer to me and I will come closer to you."*

She felt a wave of cool air pass over her, as if a nice breeze on this humid night. Startled by the soothing voice, she became angrier. Fuming, and not focused on anything but her biological father's words, she got a bit confused in the oncoming darkness and brightening neon. Her tight square jaw loosened slightly as did her fist. She felt suffocated by the ugly neon, as if all the signs were closing in on her. She turned left, right—becoming increasingly unsure of which was the right street to take home. Inside she wanted to cry—but she dared not show it, knowing what would happen for almost certain. She looked this way and that again, like a shark. She held all the emotion back, as she had so many times before. Her eyes narrowed to suspicious slits as she sought her bearings...

Fast forward: She would find her way to New York three years later; live in her Aunt's crowded hovel in Bed-Stuy Brooklyn; find her way to the Egyptian wing of the Brooklyn Museum and hear the voice of God again as she looked at the word "Maat." Again, she would hear the same words. It freaked her out and she left the museum hurriedly, carried by a cool breeze.

She would devour education while most of her cousins scorned her and spat on her for her dearth of socializing and high grades—H.S. diploma, college scholarship, masters in business administration—*nuh bumbaclaught!*—an admin job in finance, trading assistant, CFA, Risk Management license—*deny me nuh!*—Spanish fluency, altruism in community, sexism, Big Sisterhood, harassment, feeding the homeless on Christmas day, philanthropy, racism, trading sovereigns with a specialization in Pesos for Banco de Mexico before Mexico got NAFTA—no time for boys and distrusts men—and then Mexico got NAFTA and she got a brownstone in Harlem before Harlem got more blondes than Norway. And as the frat boys on the firm's trading desk will tell you, Daisy McLane won't blow you, but she got game.

Timing...

Before the candy-colored, powder-blue convertible jag with the paint job that looked so good you wanted to lick it, before reclining into the deluxe driving experience of butter-pecan-colored, Italian-leather seats and feeling the thrill of the big cat's roar, before the summer weekends on Oak Bluffs with her husband and three kids, before peering out at an aqua-marine Atlantic from her widow's walk at sunset and glancing at her diamond encrusted David Yurman watch, before all that...she found the right street on that dark night in Kingston, without asking a soul.

As she walked home the roads turned from concrete to dirt. The night sky turned from blue-gray to inky blue. She made a promise to her self. A vow. She clenched her fist. Her breathing grew heavy, like a bull. She turned her attention to what was in store for her for coming home late and causing trouble. She would take this beating like she had taken the others—without a tear. Damn them. Damn them all. Time she thought. All in a matter of time. I cannot be stopped. I refuse to be stopped. The last mile was the longest.

For Babs and Siobhan

PROSE

I... The Vulture and the Cobra

On the Vulture and the Cobra: The vulture is a symbol of protection for Upper Egypt (today's Luxor-Aswan region) and the cobra is a symbol of protection for Lower Egypt (today's Cairo-Saqarra region). Worn in the center of the pharaoh's ceremonial headdress (see any picture of Tu-tan-khamon's gleaming gold funeral mask), the symbols represent the ever watchful and potentially fiery eyes of Ra. Both symbols could come to life and strike an enemy of the pharaoh. One would poison you, then the other would eat you.

East Flatbush, Brooklyn—We were both determined not to lose. I chased Terrance into the street. An old Benz zoomed down the block. We jumped in front of it screaming like maniacs. We must have scared the hell out of that old driver.

We cut through an abandoned lot.

Huffing, I asked T, "Did you see the way Luz said 'hello' to me at the Park when we were punching out, man?"

"Rod, she ain't even know who you was. But she was all on me."

"Right," I said, "a no-talent, no-money-having JV quarterback. No, what Luz needs is someone as kool and suave as the kid."

"Knee-grow, please," T said, "Luz wants 007 not double oh no!"

The sun was setting over the cemetery, melting to a dusky, orange haze. It was about 95 degrees with no breeze. Soot coated the light-gray air. The grit slid down our throats.

"Don't tell me," T said in an English accent, "Mr. Bond is scared? Yo, man, you're debate team, Mr. Sports Editor, Mr. homeroom prez, people talkin' about you for class pres.—and we just got up in here! You're broad son! But how you gonna be that def, high-powered lawyer—getting paid in full! when you can't even kick it to a female like Luz? Buss it—tell her you're my boy, and she'll be on you like Crazy Glue."

We ran through a hollowed-out brownstone filled with charred furniture and ancient garbage.

"I'm serious, Rod," T said, grabbing me in a headlock. "Ah, payback!" he shouted into my ear. "Look! if you really like her, talk to her. You were doing pretty good for awhile that first day. If you get a second chance, just be you."

I struggled to break free but couldn't. He threw me down onto an old car seat. I tumbled off onto the rubble.

"Money!" T said, short of breath, "buss it: my boy Rod had her smiling beneath that scowl that day you worked in her group. Nobody else has been able to do that all summer." He laughed: "Except me."

I got up, chased him over the fence, down crowded Pitkin Avenue, past all the hardware, discount, and appliance stores, all of which were missing a letter here or there in their signs. I jumped and tackled him in front of Wang's Fruit and Vegetable stand, where I worked sometimes. Fruit flew everywhere. People scattered.

"Money," he kept on as we wrestled, "you're lucky I got a girl—or I'd be on her like a tattoo. She's human, just like me and you . . . a girl, just like any girl—just throw your rap!"

I got him tight around the neck, totally angered that he was right, about everything.

"Alright, alright . . ." he said, laughing.

Mr. Kim came out surveying the damage. He crossed his arms and shook his head, disappointed. "Is this harmony, boys?" he asked. "No, this is disharmony, this is chaos!" He extended his arms out to the side, pointing to all the people we'd disrupted.

"Sorry, Mr. Kim," we said simultaneously. We tossed him oranges as he juggled and skillfully placed them back onto the stands. I started telling Mr. Kim about how we'd be more careful, but T pulled me away. Mr. Wang laughed at us as we broke down the block.

Rounding the corner, we chilled out and T started talking about getting his cousin's car to go pick up my mother from the hospital, where she worked as a nurse's aid. Today she was having a check up. It would be a kool sort of surprise T thought, to pick her up in a Benz. His mother and my mother go back, to when they were girls growing up Down South, in Mecklenburg, Georgia, population 550.

I looked at my watch as we walked back to his house. Our families don't go back down South much these days. When we lived in Georgia, about 4 years ago, my maternal grandfather would put T on his shoulders and take me by the hand. We'd walk through the woods before sunrise, hiking to Indian Lake. He'd stop to define the trees—sycamores, oaks, weeping willows. We'd stop at gigantic fallen logs the size of vans, and he'd tell us stories—about Anancy the spider, big bears, kings, queens, African tales—all as night gave way to day. T and I loved those stories. Some of them were scary. Some were funny. We also loved the smell of the forest before morning, the nip in the air making the tips of our noses cold, the smell of the damp moss on trees and rocks, the wet twigs beneath our feet, the mist rolling slowly over the ground like a crush low rider.

T pulled open the screen door hanging drunk off its hinges and unlocked the backdoor. We ducked our heads to avoid hitting the dropped ceiling, bobbing between the hanging tropical plants, the hung whites dripping water onto the concrete floor and patches of curling linoleum. Potent bleach stung the air. T's mother, a general information telephone operator for the city's Labor Department, and his father, a welder with little patience for incompetence, were at work, as usual. His two sisters were probably playing two blocks away on the lower terrace of the Franklin Pierce projects, where my family lives.

T walked over to the bureau, reached into his top drawer, pulled out clean T-shirts and tossed me one. I went into the telephone-booth-size bathroom, washed up. When I got back, T was sorting and folding the clean coloreds and whites his mother had left on his bed.

Above us, small yellow track lights rimmed the margins of the white square ceiling, flicking on and off, casting shadows across the trinity of Black QB posters above T's headboard. From ceiling to floor, stacks of iron, milk-crates filled with records lined the small square room, covering, almost entirely, the royal blue walls. Black radios, big and small, lay on the deep red shag like spilled treasure. Some of the boxes had exposed faces. Multiculti wires tumbled out of others, spaghetting out onto the wall-to-wall shag. I sat down on the black beanbag in the corner and picked up one of his hand-sized experiments, a heavy walkie-talkie. T rocked the short-wave years ago, back when we were stealing candy from Pathmark. Now the boy demanded PCs and Pentium-run hardware for alchemy. (MC T, though, still able to rock any jam.)

Every other Thursday, all summer, T'd been saying, "Yo Rod we can do this. We loop with my cousin 'Rome's network, set-up some legit fronts, put a few more cops from the 7-7 on the rolls," and other bright ideas. T had the future mapped. But I knew it wasn't him talking. It was the dollar signs, steady meals, heat in the winter, no longer having to feel like a piece of shit next to the richer kids who wore designer gear and had the new Jordans first. He sounded more like his 'Rome. We had graduated from more than junior high school in June, and his cousin knew it. He also knew we were smart.

"We'll be large, boy. Yo, and buss the sweetness: no crack, no coke, purely Sertiva, Star...Look at your check, Rod, shit is lovely isn't it?"

I'd gotten us phony working papers so we could qualify for jobs as summer-youth workers at Prospect Park, although we were only 14.

He looked at the Dickensian pittance and pointed to the net. "We could make ten times this in one hour." I listened unfazed. He'd soon drop it, exasperated.

But sometimes though, I'd think about: His cousin 'Rome clocking $300,000 plus last quarter; 'Rome's 500 Benz, 'Rome's recently purchased mansion in Freeport, L.I.;'Rome's plan to exit the business in a couple of years; how the Feds could stop the flow at the source by embargoing the countries sending it in, ("Uh, but, ah, well, uh...it's just not that simple"). I'd think about how I'd probably make minimum wage again next summer, if I were lucky enough not to get busted. My mother wants me to save for college ("You've got to get ready now.") . . . She doesn't know how much of an ironic joke that is.

. . . The real deal is she just doesn't want what happened to so many of my friends, and my brother, to happen to me. That's why she tries to get me into all these programs and clubs, like, imagine, the Boy Scouts—fortune rules, fear, ivory coasts, islands of assumed safety—that's all it is.

T rested a pale yellow dress shirt on the bureau and started straightening up. The boy can't go anywhere unless his room is immaculate.

I pulled out that old Earth, Wind and Fire album, thought about the cardinal elements . . . How strong would the wind blow, what would scorch the earth, my boy? I read the liner notes: "...At the time we were making this album, people were rebelling against oppression, fighting for human rights—basic dignity."

"Yo, Cash," I said, "you ready for sophomore year?" Cash is what everyone calls T because he has a way of making money whenever he needs it.

"Yeah," he said coldly, "but if I get a fool like Thomas again—it's over." T and I took buses to a school in a safer community.

"Why not cut him some slack," I asked. "There are only two in the whole joint."

"You know the deal with Thomas," T said, "if you don't act white, and talk white, he don't want to nothing to do with you. Nigga'll send a homey to the Dean's office in a heartbeat. But be a whiteboy, or an oreo—and do the same exact thing—and everything's kool. Check out how my man acts like he's doing us some big favor—coming here from Englewood—Jersey no less, teaching us po' little black chillun."

"Yeah, " I said, "all 30 percent of us."

"Not for long," T said, meaning the school would probably be all Black in a couple of years. "...He probably figures if he can save a few 'special niggers', he's done his job." T turned back to folding, pissed.

In school, T has always had the right answers, but always wanted to discuss why they were right. Our 4th grade teacher, Mrs. Sawyer didn't like that. T, who's light-skinned, said she was racist for always punishing him for "challenging her." But I don't know. She was OK with me and I'm dark. This past year, our muscle-bound Gym teacher, Mr. Moz, had been pissed off by T, who refused to "shut up with the questions already!" Mr. Moz tried to silence T by punching him in the face, for being "disruptive." T cracked a chair over his skull, giving him a mild concussion.

T dropped a T-shirt. Picked it up. Pointed at me. "If you think I'm lying, check it: remember when I asked him how he expected me to write positive things about the 'father of our country,' the same president that owned slaves and raped Black women? Saying he 'wasn't evil'! He played my question off like I wasn't even there; just stood there fixing his fuckin' clip-on. Nah, man, I aint gettin' no flavor—stone vanilla, Money!"

All T's magazines: Science, Ebony, College Football Digest, Omni, Jet, were stacked neatly on an antique mahogany bookshelf his grandmother had left him. It had been in the family for seven generations. The magazines were in exact reverse chronological order, spines facing out. I picked up Digest, flipped though it.

"I hear you," I said. "But what do you mean, 'special niggers'?"

"Brothers," T said, "who talk and act white, or sisters who get treated like Gutamalan handbags, you know what I'm saying?"

"Oh," I said, bored, scanning the pre-season predictions in the magazine, "If you talk like you're from upstate, whether it's poor upstate or rich upsate, so long as you don't be slangin' dat slang." I smiled.

"Remember," T said, on a rant, "how Thomas was all on your tip when you told him Rodsford is a English name, and that your father's grandparents live in London? That's what he's about."

I put a house music tape in one of his boxes, pressed play. A chorus of sorrowful sopranos sang slowly: "Whoa, Whoa, Whoa" . . . then joyously, "The house lights!" behind the incoming thumping bass: "The house lights! The house lights! The house lights!" Beats came in that would make Ailey dancers go wild.

"Man?!" T said, disgusted. "Another example: say I wear hood' gear, teachers give me automatic static. Suppose I'm down with the style? That make me a hood? Myopic bullshit, man! That's what I'm telling you." He didn't say anything for awhile, just kept folding, and then murmured, " ...Thomas, wants Siamese twins." He folded a white shirt intensely—suddenly balled it, heaved it across the room toward the pail in the corner. The shirt sailed across the bed, drifting wide, missing the pail, unfurling to the floor. T turned, grabbed his football off the bureau, spun it high into the air and on his forefinger, trying to regain his calm.

"Forget Thomas, man," I said.

The drum machine on the tape rocked on, filling the silence.

Inspite of T's high scores in science and math, guidance counselors put him in classes where the handouts never made it to the second row. T'd swing by my class. We'd go shoot pool or go play video games. But we both took the placement test for this superbrain program, SPC (science, politics, and community affairs) and made it in, so we're supposed to start 3 weeks from now.

I was BSing before, the kid can throw a football. He threw 14 touchdowns and one interception in his first season. The coach raved: "Rapid release, cannon arm, and can always sense pressure before it arrives." The JV team went 8 and 1 on the strength of T's left arm. They voted him MVP of the championship game and the season. I interviewed my boy for the school paper down on the ravaged grass field. Standing under the brilliant winter sun that day, I imagined I was a fattly paid network announcer at the Super Bowl—like Bryant Musberger—and T was the MVP and a future hall of famer.

I said to T: "Where are you going now?" T smiled his toothpaste- commercial smile, looked into the camera, the whole world was watching, cheering: LOCAL BOYS MAKE GOOD... T winked, "Disney World, baby."

I slouched down into the bean bag. T caught the football in his left hand, slung it hard from hand to hand. Palmed it with each hand before letting it drop to exact depths.

After awhile I said, "Did you hear anything about the new jobs for next summer?"

"I heard they shrunk," T said: "It's only open to one person now." He folded a pair of jeans. "Probably you for the same reason I just spoke on." I could tell by his voice he wasn't coming back to the Park next summer—new job, or no new job. A 50 cent raise over minimum wasn't making it; This is like when he folded his arms across his chest and told the priest he would no longer bow before a God that did not look like him. That was about the end of our altar boy days.

"So are you down or what?" T said.

"What?" I asked, knowing it was coming to this.

"Okay, it's like that? No problem. I'll run without you." T turned back to the mirror, smoothed his fade haircut.

Now we could say when and where the road split, over bullshit—pharmaceutical sales. We could mark it on our calendars. Ten years of friendship had come down to a simple yes or no. His cousin 'Rome cashed in and would soon be cashing out, why couldn't he? Although 'Rome opposed T joining his business, he liked T's ideas and his fearlessness. What was I going to do, stand on some soapbox and say, "Oh T, please brother really, 'Just Say No.'" Emphasis on "no," a word oh so familiar.

T was supposed to be an engineer. I was going to be the lawyer. We'd be boys, forever...

Disney World, homeboy, Disney World.

My brain, like my stomach, knotted up. I slumped deeper into the beanbag, tried not to think. T had been my best friend since I could remember. We'd had the same friends, worked the same jobs, fought the same fights, a few times against crazy numbers. Was I just scared for myself?

The track lights kept blinking. I picked up a dog-eared Ebony. Astronaut Ron McNair smiled sincerely from the cover.

"So you want to be Big Time, T?!" My voice shook. I felt a surge of sadness coming up in my chest, wanting to come out as tears. "You're going to get rocked, man. Don't be fucking stupid!" A big, hollow pit grew in my stomach, a vacuum being filled by air and pain.

T rested his brush, slowly turned around from the mirror and crossed his arms.

"Funny," he said. He paused for a second... "Thomas would say, 'Let's revisit this in six months and see who's smarter—and richer!'"

"Fuck you!" I said, jumping up from the bag.

"That's very intelligent, Rod, very articulate. They're going to love that in college."

T turned back to the mirror.

Bet. I sat down, set up his chessboard. Moved a piece now and again. Rested my hand under my chin...13, 14, 15, Moustafa, Nando, Popo, Vance, Shak, 21, 22...How many of my friends would not live to be 18? Now my boy Terrance. Terrance LaMar Hunter. 23.

The keys to 'Rome's Benz rattled around in his pocket.

"Ready?" T asked. He stepped over to me. Looked down at the board, moved the black bishop to the right: "Check-mate, Money."

I got up. "Dip!" I said, surprised, like nothing had happened. "That was nice!"

"Twice as nice, boy." He smiled. I hit the top of his fist.

Just then everything seemed normal, like before.

T stooped to loosen his sleek new tennis sneakers, all white Stan Smiths. How many more times would I see him? Would the next time be on the six o'clock news, clutching a windbreaker over his face, flanked by cops? Maybe on Flatbush Avenue, face down, his blood spilling out onto the concrete, like what happened to Big Dave and Popeye? Or maybe I would have to I.D. his cracked out body at the morgue, and then go ring his mother's bell . . .

For real . . .

I looked at my best friend, my key boy since I could remember, and knew I wouldn't see him past 12th grade. When he walked out, he would be alone, a shadow on the street.

It won't work T! School is the fight! That's a sucker trap, man. We can bust out this bullshit SPC program. Trust me—it ain't NO thing!

But it was too late for all that, and only words, words he'd heard before. He took a final look around the room, making sure everything was in order. He noticed the white shirt that had fallen, picked it up, held it up to the blinking lights, shifted it to the left, to the right, scrutinizing it for cleanliness. He folded it neatly and put it in the garbage.

We walked out into the bright afternoon sunlight and jumped in the gleaming black Benz.

"So, what's up, Capone?" T said sarcastically. "I can see those wheels spinning."

I hated when he called me by my old thug name. Yeah, I had done my dirt, felt the blood of my enemies splash back on me. The images of my violence flashed back in my mind for a second like a quick cuts of a horror movie, and for a minute I couldn't believe it was me that had done that damage. Our crew had been large. Then gradually there was only T and I. The smart and the lucky. By junior high, everybody was in Spoffard, Rikers or, as T would say, had caught a mad vapor to the dome.

"You want to know what's on my mind," I said, pissed off, "You're talking about short paper. Why do you need a Gulf Stream when you can fly first class? I'm talking about long paper. It takes longer to get, but it lasts a lot longer and you live a lot longer. Your way, you get fat quick, but you probably die quick. Check this, T: You know our supervisor Mike at the park, his homeless hippie look is all a front. His father works in the City in the office of Budget and Finance. Instead of taking that seed money to open up a weed spot, break him off a proper chunk. In return, I'll tell him to get you, me and Luz jobs in the office of Budget and Finance. Those jobs pay three times more, and look dope on college applications. Just hear me out. Second, instead of doing high school in 3 years, we speed this up and finish it this year. Double up on all the courses we need at a night school, intersession and over the summer at night, take the SATs now, bust those out and go to college at 16. We only need a little more than one year of courses anyway, because we're in SPC. Third, what's the powerhouse college football program in the tri-state area?

"There is none," he said, intrigued.

"Of course there isn't, but there is an Ivy League school up in Harlem, and they're dying for some brothers who can ball.

T waved it off, "Please. The Ivy league can't ball."

"Exactly. Since you've been busting it out, you get the coach to have the Columbia coach come down and check you out. Shit, big name schools are already talking about checking you out, so why not get a degree from a big name school that's going to open doors for you and you know with your skills—you will start. You're blue chip, and everyone and their momma knows it. So buss it! We do this program in four quarters. The first quarter will be rough. Each quarter after that will be easier. If by the second quarter everything isn't falling like I said, then you can put a cap in me! Give me one year. I will have you in a job paying three times what your making now, in an Ivy league school playing Varsity—because those kids haven't had a winning season since the flood—with your tuition paid for and more, and then, bam—do your time at Columbia, expedite that in 3 years, you're 19, with an Ivy league degree headed to an engineering firm or Wall Street making sweet six figures with the potential to make much more. Or fuck the dumb shit, stay at Columbia for the MBA, rack a nice salary in the summer between your first and second year, and then hit the street at 21 with a bachelors and masters from an Ivy League school. Fuck with it." I said. "if the academics and playing ball get too rough. I'll carry you. You know we've done that before."

He hit my fist, laughed: "Fucking Capone. Always thinking. Alright man, I'll give you're words some thought."

"Fuck that!" I said, "the name of this game is speed. Either you are down and we start making this program happen today by going to see Mike, or you chase that short paper and let me know how it works out. Speak!"

"This brotha," T said, shaking his head. He didn't like being pressed. He preferred to do the pressing. After a few minutes he said, "Four quarters?"

"Give me two. If its not flowing lovely, I'll work two jobs to give you back the money you put out. That's word bond! You know I control the media in that school. I'll send out press releases to every paper in the City until you're a bigger phenom than you are now. And you know I can do it. I'll have the New York Times down on that field."

He laughed again, slapping the steering wheel. "My boy. Let's go pick up your moms, man." I knew he was thinking about all the robberies of crooked storeowners I had engineered when we were younger, and how my crime track record was flawless. I knew if he accepted most of the work would be on me.

"We can call my mother. Business first," I said, serious as cancer.

The Benz slowly rolled right, like a cloud toward Prospect Park.

For Debbie Cozier, with my sincerest apologies

PROSE

2... Train of Thot

On Thot: In Egyptian spirituality, Thot is the ibis-headed god of knowledge, writing and divine speech (which in part means to speak truth from your heart and let truth cling to your lips). Lord of books, scribe of the gods and patron of all writers, he created oral and written communication. Thot invented: the Egyptian language; astronomy; astrology; mummification; the Egyptian mystery system (called the Ka-ba-la in its watered down form) that all pharaohs and priests had to master; as well as meditation; mathematics (e.g., algebra, geometry and calculus); and medicine (e.g., from nutrition to post-op rehab). Measurer of the earth and counter of the stars, Thot kept and recorded all data. Thot authored critical religious texts, such as *The Book of Coming Forth By Day,* aka *The Book of the Dead.* When the deceased reached the underworld's hall of judgment, Thot read all of the person's deeds. When you read the tarot, he created the symbols that you see. For those who know the ancient Egyptian Mystery System, the meanings of the tarot symbols are clear. For those who are uninitiated, such as the ancient Romans and Greeks, the symbols remain a mystery.

As we waited on the empty platform for the Brooklyn/ Southbound A train, I noticed a group of boys leaping like frogs over the concrete railing, one after the other, about 25 of them.

"Go on the other side," I said to the little girl sitting next to me, "and take the train one stop and then switch sides and take it back." She walked quickly toward the stairs with her head down, pigtails dangling at the sides. *If they even think about touching her, there will be much blood on the tracks today!* A murderous intensity swelled in my chest at the thought of them even saying one word to her. This intensity made me itch to break bones at thought of all the black women raped in slavery, Sally Hemmings included! How I wanted to smack the shit out of my history teacher who told me Sally Hemmings was Thomas Jefferson's "mistress." Rather than resort to violence, I had told him the legal definition was "chattel," and more to the point "rape." He made a face and moved on, but without the smile on his face at recounting the "forbidden love" story between Hemmings and slave-owner president Thomas Jefferson.

The leader—a skinny kid in jeans, blue polyester track jacket, white T-shirt and flat gold chain—started in on me as soon as he spotted me. His geek chorus followed his lead. As they shouted, I remembered why people call Howard Beach, Queens, "Coward Beach." (Last year, two black bus drivers eating dinner in a pizzeria were chased onto the Grand Central Parkway by a "wolf pack" of wilding youths, to quote the press.) Coward Beach was also home to the now dead "Dapper Don," former New York Mob boss John Gotti, a premier drug trafficker revered by the many of the neighborhood kids because he symbolized to them strength, power and benevolence.

Surrounded and barraged by their racial insults, my view quickly became dark. The air became hotter than an oven on Thanksgiving Day. I felt like the air was being choked off and it became difficult to breathe. I decided to drag the first one to hit me onto the tracks and kill him as bloodily as possible, which might scare the others off, as had proved to be the case in the past. I doubted if many of them wanted to fight me on the tracks. They seemed like punks, and it was a 5-story drop to the speeding traffic.

I stared into the leader's beady blue eyes: "If you hit me," I said, "it's on." They all leaned in closer and amplified the verbal barrage, daring him to hit me.

I pressed my sweaty palms into my thighs. I was outnumbered, so I had to chill until one of them decided to set it. Sweat from Brooklyn's July humidity soaked the back of my T-shirt.

. . . *Picture those bus drivers, trying to escape in the winter night, running for their lives, losing all sense of where they were, jumping over the railing, running into oncoming headlights, cars zooming at them. What did their screams sound like when the first cars severed their bodies?*

As I listened to the leader dis my mom, my family, my "race," I looked into his glacial eyes and felt that if I clutched his neck, I could snap it with one hand. *Stay chill* I said to myself, *No blood, no foul. This is not your first time at the rodeo, just EZ* . . .So I sat there looking out, beyond them, bored, indifferent, as if waiting for a train on a lazy summer afternoon.

The leader was dying to see me flinch, cower—show some sign of fear. But I couldn't give it up. I wasn't scared. I had accepted my death as soon as I had counted more than 20 of them jumping over the concrete railing. Time for my 15 minutes of fame, my mug on the cover of the *New York Post*, I joked to myself. The leader and his friends continued loudly explaining, in myriad detail, how they were going to kill me, stomp me, snatch my gold, my watch, kick all my teeth in, etc. . . . I wondered what they were waiting for. For a second, I thought this situation was ironic, because some people don't think I'm black enough, because I'm the color of pine, or what some kids at my school call "high yellow." My father had always said not to let intraracial taunts phase me: "Look at W.E.B. Dubois or Tom Joyner, who were light-skinned—or even Malcom X, who was a red-bone—and it was a brown-skinned man that had assassinated him. It's not about color. It's never been about color. It's about an artificial construct created to facilitate the economic empowerment of one culture over many others. It's about commitment to culture and pride in heritage. . . .It's about heart! It's about character. Color is only used for profits, to divide and conquer. Distract and destroy."

Some kids would tell me I didn't speak "black" enough, as if all blacks speak the same way or all use urban slang. I had to have fights with hard rocks on the back of the school bus just because I wanted to read a book on the way to school, because if I was reading I was, of course, "trying to be white." But I fought those fights, and got my respect. I decided that if I had gone from being wild to mild, people still had to respect me, and I would fight for that respect against black, white or whomever.

Now I was being told I wasn't light enough, although my mother was half-white, or bi-racial.

Often I wondered where I fit in, with my black friends, with my white friends, or with my friends who could see past color. It got confusing a lot. I was trying to be cool with everyone and wound up being distrusted by everyone because I was seen always hanging with the wrong crew. So now I hang by myself.

I stared through the punks surrounding me, to the station in the distance, to another day, to the light you enter when beaming toward heaven or hell, to Thot, the ibis-headed Egyptian god of writing, who records all your life's deeds. His partner in the underworld, the jackal-headed god Anubis, escorts the dead to their trial by the lord and judge of the underworld, Osiris. The goddess Maat, symbolized as a feather, is used by Osiris to judge your deeds. Maat is the goddess of truth, justice and order. The jackal-headed Anubis, your guide through the underworld, places the feather of Maat on one side of a legal scale and your heart on the other. All of your actions are read aloud by Thot and placed on the scale. Anubis asks you first 42, then 125 moral questions, similar to the 10 commandments. If you tell Osiris the correct answers you will go to the Elysian Fields, an Eden-like place where you will chill with Osiris. If your heart is heavier than the feather, Anubis throws you into a flaming abyss filled with starving alligators, whose jaws are snapping ferociously. You go to the Elysian Fields if you can become a god while you are still a man. That is, the beauty of the Elysian Fields are in you, if you know you to tap it, be it, live it. Finding the Elysian Fields within is what the ancient Egyptian priests taught their young initiates. It is how you attain Heaven on Earth; and what reggae artist Bob Marley meant when he sang, "a mighty god is a living man." The bridge from man to God is the most difficult one to find and the easiest to cross, depending on the level of your commitment. One of the questions is "Have you ever committed violence?" I would have to sadly answer yes, pray for forgiveness and hope that I had done some things to balance those times out. I pictured my bloody heavy heart on the scale…

Started thinking about the fight to come on the tracks, pressure points, cracking skulls on rails, the free fall to the street. I heard on long falls you die from fright before impact. Your heart gives out as you see what's approaching.

Hearts jackhammering through their official bus-company shirts, stomachs cramping from exhaustion, sweat pouring down their faces, open mouths gasping for what they hope will not be last breaths, limping, but still running, running on fumes and desperation. In the cold night air, they hear the footsteps closing in on them, certain death, a mob of angry boys with guns and bats and hate of the unknown. The bus drivers push their bodies to the breaking point, wheezing from shortness of breath. They are lost, disoriented, frosty clouds of air gust from their mouths, evaporating in the night. A fear like they never imagined grips them, full blown from the pit of their stomachs, overtaking their entire bodies—then they jump—over the highway's guardrail, hoping, flying to another place.

I had already decided that I wasn't going to run from this wolf pack—and I damn sure wasn't going out alone!

The northbound train pulled in. The little girl got on. I felt a huge sigh of relief.

The lord of the shit flies continued talking trash and feigning blows to my face. He lunged for my gold rope with the platinum Ankh—the ancient Egyptian cross, the symbol of vital energy, the fusion of male and female energy; the symbol of eternity, life, and fertility—but he stopped just short, as if he were waiting for me to react, so they could all legitimately stomp me. I looked through him as if he were invisible, man.

After about 25 minutes of this, his key boy said to him, "Why don't you chill out," and most of them started to drift to the other end of the platform, leaving just me and the young Klansman-wannabe. . . .

The southbound train pulled in. The last car stopped in front of us. The doors opened. Ganja wafted out, followed by deep voices and competing boxes booming straight gangsta rap. I stood up. The circle surrounding me parted like the Red Sea.

I held the door open for the leader, motioning with my arm for him to enter first. His mouth fell open as he looked at the hard and scarred muscle-bound brothers, who stopped smoking blunts, stared at him with eye-narrowing hatred, as if they knew in an instant what had went down. The leader's boys lost color. Their mouths dropped open, as if attached to dumb bells. The brothers turned down the boxes, having all been in (or heard about) similar situations. You could feel the tension rise exponentially. Now the sides were even. Shit was about to get evil. They looked at me, looked at my frozen tormentors and moved to the edge of their seats, waiting for any word or action from me.

"After you," I said to the leader. But, surprisingly, he now had nothing to say. He was perhaps drinking in new lessons about what the ancient Egyptian God Ra calls *manhood, reciprocity* and *grace*?

"Is something wrong?" I asked sarcastically, as Ra told me what to do. "Why, you're so quiet now." I smiled to the leader, "Come on," and waved him in again, as if to say *The water's fine, come on in.* I slapped him on the back and he fell forward onto the train then quickly stepped back out.

I laughed as the conductor shouted over the PA: "Release the doors!" I just shook my head at the leader, "Exactly what I thought. You're a big man with your boys, but a punk now. Pathetic. Just another punk-ass racist." I feigned a punch at him and he flinched.

The little girl who had gone north and then came back south, bolted from her seat, pig tails flying, jumped up at the leader and spat in his face: "Who's the nigger now?" She punched her little fists on her hips and snarled her question again when he didn't answer. He wiped the saliva from his eye, and grimaced. She kicked him in the shin and tossed her pigtail like an angry little diva, shrieking the question again. She had seen everything before getting on the train.

One of the brothers—Golden Gloves shredded—ripped off his green nylon A-shirt, and got up into the leader's face, his cannon-ball shoulders heaved forward ominously: "She asked you a question, bitch!" which made the leader back up against the concrete wall, shrink and cower. None of his boys moved to help him.

I lifted her back in, "Come on, Toughie." The brother waited for a response then spat hard in the leader's eye: "You bitch-ass nigger!" The brother backed up into car, looking at them like they would never earn their nuts. I let the doors go. The brothers eased back into their seats. The music was turned back up, spliffs were re-lit.

"Niggers!" the brother who had taken off his shirt spat out with venom. He returned to his seat and puffed hard on a blunt, slowly shaking his head back and forth. In prison, the lines are thick and racial, not that much different from outside of prison.

I could easily have dragged the "man for all seasons" inside, and that would have been the end of him, "a moveable feast," to quote the author of the racist short story, "The Killers." When I was 13 or 14—before I converted to the forerunner of Christianity, the ancient Egyptian spiritual belief system known as Maat, which is based on order, justice and truth—I would have yanked him in and stomped his head like a grape, without any hesitation. Before finding Maat, or before Maat found me, I left Converse imprints on kids' skulls as my daily signature. I was, after all, a Jolly Stomper gang member at age 11. During those times, my father couldn't reach me. But that was then, and now, my fight was not these brothers' fight, and if the leader's key boy had backed his play to the fullest, I might be dead now. And what do they say about the value of *talk*?. . . Why escalate it to murder when no one had touched me? Controlling my emotions, fear as well as anger, was something Maat had taught me, keep everything in emotional balance, success as well as failure, life is peaks and valleys, know yourself, control yourself—"Order: internal discipline and development"—Order, being one of the seven principles of Maat. The others being Justice: be fair to all in your actions; Balance: the right measure in all good things; Harmony: righteousness and generosity in community; Propriety: loyalty and service to those respected; Reciprocity: do for another so he or she may also do; and Truth: speak it from you heart, let it cling to your lips.

The brothers on this train would have broken their 40s beer bottles all over that kid's head and shredded him with glass, box cutters and vicious 007 knives. The coroner would not be able to identify him; there would be no dental records. And perhaps, I would not be the only one going to jail for murder. That would be unjust, unbalanced. I had proven my point about their characters. I would release them to the universe and their fates, which I knew to be cruel.

The train blew steam and chugged forward. In the next car, I sat next to the little girl, who tossed a braided pig tail and said sarcastically, "That's the Sally Hansen crew for ya." Sally Hansen makes nail hardener for girls. In Brooklyn, when a guy is trying to act hard but is really soft, kids say, "Here comes Sally Hansen, hard as nails."

For Colette

PROSE

3...Paula and David

On the Pyramids *"Man fears time. Time fears only the pyramids,"* ancient proverb. With the exception of the sphinx, the pyramids on the Giza Plateau are the only wonders from the ancient world that still stand. The pyramids rise up like flames to the sun. They are symbols of natural balance, harmony and triads in life.

The pyramid is a burial chamber, so when you go to Egypt don't climb them, although the attendants may ask you if you'd like to. A pyramid is meant to be an everlasting structure to house the pharaoh's everlasting spirit/ka (as his ba/mirror spirit ascends from a portal in the pyramid to the Heavens on a ray of light). Many of the more than 50 pyramids found by archaeologists have burial chambers seven stories below surface level. In Egypt, they say it is not a matter of building high, but building deep.

The pyramids of Giza are comprised of two-ton (and heavier) stones that are precisely cut and interlocked. How were those stones cut in those ancient times? What tools could have cut those two-ton blocks so precisely? How was the stone quarried? The mortar used is of an unknown origin. It has been analyzed and it's chemical composition is known but it can't be reproduced. It is stronger than the stone.

In the spiritual center of Egypt, Abydos, there is a temple with hieroglyphs depicting modern airplanes and helicopters.

This was a society that was so far advanced that today we cannot fully comprehend it. Has time regressed? Or is destiny being fulfilled?

Originally, the pyramids were covered by a layer of smooth white limestone and crowned by a sheet of gold at the apex. The centers of the four sides of the great pyramid are indented with an extraordinary degree of precision forming the only eight-sided pyramid. The effect is not visible from the ground or from a distance, but only from the air.

The word "pyramid" is from the Greek words "pyra" meaning fire, light, or visible, and the word "midos" meaning measures. The mathematical concepts pi, phi and the Pythagorean theorem were all used in building the great pyramid. Pi is the principal relationship between the great pyramid's height and base. Pi expresses the natural law of the mystical trinity wherein three infinite components are contained in one

Thus, there are three pyramids on the Giza Plateau and one sphinx. Three pharaohs created the Giza pyramids and they all came from one dynastic line, one blood line.

As the great pyramid is perfectly aligned to north, south, east and west, so the sphinx is perfectly aligned to the four cardinal elements. The sphinx also represents the three and one concept. The sphinx is one mass cut from the bedrock of the Giza Plateau. The mystery of the sphinx is that the sphinx is God/Ausar/Osiris represented as man/all things. First, the head of the sphinx is god's representative on Earth, the pharaoh or the anointed savior/Jesus Christ/Aquarius/ability to reason/heaven/cardinal sign air/yang. Second, the sphinx's body is that of a lion/Leo/cardinal sign fire/yang. Third, the sphinx's chest is the breast of woman, symbolizing Virgo/the Virgin Mary/cardinal sign earth/yin; and the cardinal sign water is symbolized by the annual Nile flooding/zodiac sign pieces/ the last sign of the zodiac, which encompasses all signs and cleanses and dissolves all things/yin/the hero, the avenger, hours, heru, the hero. Thus, in the sphinx, we find perfect harmony and balance. Three in one, and three and one. Universal Love. Or, what it means to be the rock of ages.

Pi et al. were later "discovered" by the Greeks in late B.C. The Greek, Alexander the Great, conquered Egypt in 330 B.C. In so doing, he looted and burned the massive library in what is now called Alexandria. The burning of the books destroyed most of the knowledge of the Egyptians and their mystery system.

With its golden capstone in place, the great pyramid could be seen from the mountains in Israel and the moon. Its polished hard limestone surfaces reflected light like a beacon.

Some data: The average temperature of Egypt equals the average temperature of Earth, which equals the temperature of the Queen's Chamber in the great pyramid: 68 degrees Fahrenheit. With the original surrounding courtyards and temples in place, the pyramid was used as a sundial and to indicate solstices and equinoxes. The great pyramid is the most accurately aligned structure in existence and faces true north with only 3/60th of a degree of error. The position of the North Pole moves over time and the pyramid was probably exactly aligned at one time. The great pyramid is located at the center of the land mass of the earth. The east/west parallel that crosses the most land and the north/south meridian that crosses the most land intersect in two places on Earth, one in the ocean and the other at the great pyramid. The length of a base side of the great pyramid is 9,131 pyramid inches measured at the mean socket level, or 365.24 pyramid cubits, which is the number of days in a year. The perimeter of the base divided by 100 equals 365, the number of days in a year. The length of the great pyramid's antechamber, used as the diameter of a circle, produces a circumference of 365.242. The ratio of the lengths of the Grand Gallery to the solid diagonal of the King's Chamber times 100 equals the number of days in a year. The average height of land above sea level for the Earth is 5,449 inches. This is also the height of the great pyramid.

The entire Giza Plateau is a monument to light. The great pyramid contains in its many dimensions all of the median "measures" of light. The great pyramid is located at 29 degrees 58 minutes 51 seconds north latitude (according to our present system of measurement). There is a direct correlation between light speed and the Great Pyramid's latitude: a) 29 degrees; b) 58 minutes of arc is 97% of one degree; c) 51 seconds of arc is 85% of one minute of arc. Those numbers together: 29 97 85 or 299,785, is the speed of light in meters per second. The latitude of the great pyramid transposed approximates our present measurement of the Speed of Light (in meters) in a vacuum. The number 29.9785 is also related to the age of Jesus Christ at the time of his illumination and baptism by John the Baptist ("almost" 30 years: "I am the light.")

The pyramid positions on the Giza Plateau reflect three of the positions of stars in the constellation Orion (read: Osiris), circa 10,400 B.C. Five of the 7/seven brightest stars in the constellation have pyramid equivalents: The three pyramids on the Giza Plateau form the belt of Orion; while the pyramid of Nebka at Abu Rawash corresponds to the star Saiph, and the pyramid at Zawat al Aryan corresponds to the star Bellatrix.

If the great pyramid were a clear crystal or glass prism, it would reflect sunlight at an angle of about 26.5 degrees. The descending passage in the great pyramid has an angle of approximately 26.30 degrees. The great pyramid marks the spring equinox by not marking it. That is, due to the angle of the sides of the pyramid versus its latitude, it casts no shadow at noon during the spring equinox.

There is so much stone mass in the pyramid that the interior temperature is constant and equals the average temperature of the Earth, 68 degrees Fahrenheit. The Giza Plateau has a fairly level granite bedrock base, in essence, a flat topped mountain. Other regions near the great pyramid could not have supported the immense weight of the structure. Until the 19th century the great pyramid was the tallest structure on Earth.

Most pyramids were accompanied by smaller satellite pyramids usually built to the south and east of the main pyramid. Some were tombs for queens and princesses. Most of the structures were mastabas built to entomb the pharaoh's family, members of royalty, and the priestly class.

When you go the pyramids you will stand where the great ones stood. You will stand where pharaohs stood with their architects and designed destiny. You will feel a connection with the ancient past. You will feel firmly rooted in the modern present and you will have a keen sense of your place in the hi-tech future. Welcome to the place where man meets God.

[The phone rings. David pauses the DVD player, gets up from the couch and searches for the phone in the slightly rundown, but stylishly decorated studio apartment. It is a huge box with high ceilings, and Sheik-like décor, yet it is also very hi-tech mod. A gigantic flat screen TV rests on unvarnished dark-wood floors surrounded by speakers that would make Dolby envious. The silver surround-sound stereo system pumps out the intro music to Monday Night Football. David was lounging on his sleek, long black leather couch drinking a Stella lager and watching the DVD, waiting for the game to come on. Opposite the couch is a 6-foot rectangular fish tank filled with 2 non-man-eating piranha, as well as other brightly colored tropical fish. The piranhas look harmless. Keeping the fish healthy and watching them swim is David's pride and joy. He glances at them and smiles. He likes watching them with the lights dimmed while contemplating his recently failed 3-year relationship. David can't find the cordless phone and decides to ignore it. He turns back on his movie and ignores the ringing. The ringing stops... then starts again.]

Paula: Hey, what's up little brother?

David: Hey, not a whole lot, Paula, just watching a video.

P: Oh, yeah, which one?

D: This French movie called *Thieves* with Catherine Deneuve. [David hits stop and C-Span coverage of a senate investigation hearings appears.]

P: Oh yeah, is it good?

D: Oh, yeah, she plays this professor trying to get her life sorted. You gotta see this one scene where she riffs on her old relationship to her ex, this "perfect boyfriend" type—you know the type, everything I'm not: tall, a doctor, easy on the eyes. But it seems Doctor Love didn't have the prescription for orgasms, so he got dropped like Algorithms 485; and she picked up a cutie co-ed who didn't need a road map to find her G-spot.

P: [*laughs a little*]

I & I

D: Deneuve asks Mr. Perfect to think about what makes a relationship meaningful (instead of continually dissing her economically poor, but emotionally rich, current lover as "trash"—especially since he doesn't even know Deneuve's lover, you know?).

P: Sounds like a good movie.

D: Oh, yeah. Deneuve tells him that their relationship died because there was no threat of physical violence; and I quote, "if there is no threat of physical violence in a relationship, the relationship has no point."

[Because David is cynical and jaded, he gets tired of glancing at the old men sitting behind the microphones and green felt-covered tables. He switches to his favorite channel, the Weather channel. He lowers the sound to barely audible. The beautiful brown weather woman says, "Tonight there will be variable cloudiness with a dense fog moving in around midnight. Showers will arrive around noon time and continue through the remainder of the week...."]

P: Whether it's a mother and a child, or a husband and a wife, you have to be emotionally invested at a certain level to make any relationship important. But you have to know where the thin—

D: black and blue

P: line is.

D: But when a person is in a heated argument, what turns it into a fight, ya know? What makes all the caring and passionate love—the high emotional investment you're talking about—what makes that explode from a fist, or worse. Is the trigger a revealed infidelity, insulting a mother, being selfish in bed, spending too much at Bloomingdale's with his or her gold card, what? What truly justifies hitting a person?

P: [*in a low timid voice*] I don't know. [...after a few seconds, in a normal voice] To be honest, I've wanted to hit him, but he's so much bigger than me. He'd murder me.

D: I wonder if there are some women who feel they deserve to be hit?

P: I don't know.

D: I don't know either. . . . Maybe there are some women who feel they need to be hit because they provoked their men to a certain boiling point. And I know "men" who believe you have to hit a woman every now and then "to let her know who's boss"; and I thank them, because their women come running straight to me; and I think some women take the abuse because they believe their husbands truly love them, and the hits happen infrequently. These are women I feel really sorry for. They weren't taught to value themselves. They weren't taught to expect much from life. They probably think that all men are abusive, regardless of education level and income, so why not stay with this one, at least he doesn't hit me all the time.

[silence... David reaches for the remote and turns to BET (Black Entertainment Television) where the 50-person Baptist choir is singing "Nothing but the righteous shall make heaven"; David wonders if he has come off sounding self-righteous. And dismisses that thought: *not me I'm a modern, down-to-earth man, concerned more with soul than Saab*]

P: Have you ever hit a woman?

D: No. But I came close.

P: What happened?

D: She hit me. But I told her I wasn't going to play into her sterotype of the violent Black male and walked away. I told when she was ready to discuss our problems like a rational adult I would be ready, willing and able. And then I left.

P: What happened when you came back?

D: She was OK. We talked about it and got it sorted. I think if you are a real player you should be able to break your woman down intellectually, mentally, if that is what you think it takes. Everybody knows psychological abuse is much worse than physical abuse. The scars are more lasting.

D: But if these abusive guys—and I say *guys* because these are not *men*—wanted to "control" their women, they would learn how to understand their women, learn how to talk to them—learn how to love them! In every sense of the word! [angrier] But these guys—from my experience—only think women are good for one thing, which is why their relationships are always cheap! . . . I'm sorry, I'm ranting.

P: He never hit me.

D: I'm sorry...Do you ever tell yourself the truth?

P: That is the truth!

D: Me thinks the lady doth protest too much. . . .

[Silence for a minute]

D: Do you think you'll know when to walk away from an argument with him, before it gets too heated—or when to walk away from this marriage, before it gets too ugly, even if only for a trial separation?

P: He hasn't hit me [choked with emotion and memory] . . . He's only threatened to hit me. [She flashes back to the first time he grabbed her by her long hair and threw her to the floor, slamming into the wall, barely missing hitting her head on the radiator.]

D: When I visited you last month, I saw what was behind your sunglasses, and it wasn't glamorous. I wanted to kick his ass, but nooo, you were like, "No, no, it wasn't like that. It was just an accident"—bullshit. If that motherfucker touches you again, I'm coming down there and breaking him in half!

[Silence for 15 or so seconds. . . .a smile crosses her face as she entertains that idea.]

[David switches the channel to the 1950's *Lawrence Welk Show.* Two couples in purple tie and tails are tap dancing to that

light champagne music. Very Fred Astaire and Ginger Rodg-
ers. David wonders if the rate of abuse was this high in the 50s,
when the majority of women didn't work.]

P: I don't know. . . . I don't know what I should do. He just
turns his back to me when I try to talk to him or grunts, "Make
it quick!" He comes home, watches wrestling or football, and
that's it. He doesn't want to make love unless he's drunk and has
watched the Playboy channel for a few hours, and then there's
nothing tender about it. I haven't had an orgasm in three years.

D: [Surprised.] You've been married for three years. So before the marriage, did you enjoy sex with him?

P: Yes. But it was much different when we were dating. He
really wanted to please me, now he could care less, so long as he
gets an orgasm. But sex is not the most important thing. When
you love someone, sex is not the most important thing. You
make allowances and hope that other things will come in time. I
just wanted to be with him so bad. . . . When we got engaged, he
promised to help me cook and clean, since we were both working and I was also going to school at night. But he hasn't done
anything! It's just the opposite! He's a total slob and expects me
to clean up after him—like a slave, going around picking up his
dirty socks. All he does is eat, fart and watch television. When
I argue with him about it, he says, "What *me*—clean up? Why
did I get married then?" To be honest, things have been going
down hill since our honeymoon: he never wanted to make love;
all he did on the cruise was get drunk to cure his toothache.
And then he wanted me to get this cute dentist we met to come
to our room to look in on him!

D: God!…So I guess a marriage counselor is out of the question?

P: I'm going to see a psychologist on Thursday. I'm totally stressed out. I've asked him to see a marriage counselor with me, but he says he doesn't have any problems. He's like: "Everything was fine before you wanted to talk all the time." He finally said OK to the marriage counselor, but then blew off the appointment. I don't know . . . Maybe I should take up martial arts or yoga, or something, get out some of this aggression out before I displace it. After he hit me that first time, I was *so* shocked, I just lay on the floor, I felt intimidated, scared, then I just ran out of the house. He ran after me apologizing like crazy, but it happened again. The second time, he twisted my hair into a knot and pulled it so hard I started to bleed in my scalp. [Paula feels ashamed to admit that the man she had introduced to her whole family as the man she loves, like no other, leaves her with black eyes. This idea was hard to come to grips with, the words were even harder to say. She would never admit this to anyone but David.] The fights happen twice a year now.

D: I wouldn't call them fights.

P: I know I can expect them twice a year, just like Thanksgiving and Christmas, and right around those times. [She pictures her drunken husband grumbling at the Thanksgiving table, "Your mother is to blame for all our problems! She's always hated me, from the very beginning; I wasn't white-collar enough, rich enough, small enough! She's always hated me!]

D: [Says between clenched teeth] Do you still love him?

P: Not anymore, and I've told him this. Many times.

D: Do you think because he hits you, he cares about you? [He switches from Lawrence Welk to a hip-hop video on MTV]

P: No, I used to think so, but now I realize that it's a pride thing, he doesn't want to be spoken back to, especially about his mother, Oh, I can't say a word about his mother—when she's not hitting the vodka she's a saint, which is what I told him . . . [quietly] that's the first time he hit me. . . . I realize now that he gets threatened very easily. It's like you asked me at the beginning—you've had a lot of girlfriends: does a relationship have a point, if it doesn't have the threat of violence?

D: [seething] What does he say when you tell him you don't love him?

P: He says, "That's OK, I love *you*. And I'll never give you a divorce."

D: Do you know what his other hot buttons are?

P: [Biting her nail] Yes.

[The hip-hop video shows a group of girls lounging poolside before fading to a shot of a girl grieving in the street over the bullet-riddled body of her boyfriend. She very gracefully covers his head with her pink shawl. The video, "The Wheel of Fortune (Keeps on Spinning)" ends as the word "spinning" echoes endlessly, before finally fading into a new video: that creamy black & white video of the soul singer, Sade (pronounced *sha-day*), atop the Chrysler building, looking quite buff with her underwear-model abs and dancing slow and groovy, singing "Cherish the Day" with honey-soaked soprano vocals: ". . . This is my prayer, if you were mine, I wouldn't want to go Heaven. . . .Show me how deep love can be."]

D: Good, don't push those buttons. He's manic-depressive. [David wonders how much Paula would weep if her husband suddenly died; David wonders what it would take for her to be fed up, and why his sister has always had such a large capacity for forgiveness, while he has zero.] I can't believe how in denial he is about the state of your marriage. Have you weighed the pros and cons of being single?

P: I have. But I feel like I've invested six years in this relationship and. . .and, and to be completely honest, I don't, I don't want to be alone.

D: I can only imagine the emotional toll ending this marriage might take on you, Paula. Please know I'm here for you, no matter what! And don't worry, everything will work out, OK? You're a smart, beautiful woman with a strong spirit. You have so much going for you. Whatever you decide to do, you'll come out on top. That's word bond—and you know it. Don't cry. He's not worth your tears. You've cried enough for him.

P: OK.

D: I know you've invested a lot of time in this marriage, but maybe six years are better than eight? And if you and he had children—and I realize there *were* or *are* times, or there are times when he can seem like a good guy—what kind of message would you be sending to your little girl, or your little boy, if they saw you being beaten? Does he have a gun in the house?

P: No. I've thought about how it would affect the children. And I've thought about the fights our parents had. I've wondered if I'm duplicating mom's life: being with a man who is stubborn and volatile.

D: The difference is that dad never hit mom. He was a rager, sure, but he never hit her. And I'm sure with your Miss America good looks, you've still got a large fan club. So I doubt if you would be alone for more than a second. I'm sure those guys at your bank would love it if you were suddenly single.

P: [Distressed at the prospect of dating, having to sort through the losers and gropers.]

D: Do you think any of his complaints against you are valid?

P: Now that he's making money he wants this very traditional wife who stays at home and cooks and cleans, but that's not what we agreed to before we got married. But now, he has a very selective memory, and he doesn't remember anything about our earlier conversations. I want to live, you know. I don't want to be cooped up like a lot of my friends. I want to always learn new things, take classes all the time. You know how much I love school.

D: I know. He doesn't know how good he has it. Wait till he marries a bimbo who just wants him for his money, and believe me that's what up next for his stupid ass. She'll stay at home alright. . . . Do you trust him? Or do you think he's having an affair?

P: I trust him. I know he's not having an affair. But I went to this fortune-teller that my friend highly recommended—

D: Oh, no.

P: Oh, yes! Don't scoff. She said he was having an affair with "a dark-haired woman." And one day, I noticed him putting on a brand new shirt and getting all dolled up—and he never buys anything. When I asked him about it, he denied it and became very embarrassed. I just laughed. I told him, "I *wish* you were having an affair." A few weeks later, I noticed long strands of black hair on his shirt as I was pulling it out of the hamper.

D: Are *you* having an affair?

P: God—*I* wish. I guess I could have one very easily.

D: Do you want to get separate bank accounts?

P: I did that last week. I don't want him to think—even for a minute—that I married him for his money. But I want to be able to say that I did everything I could to save this marriage. He was totally fine with getting separate accounts. If we do get divorced I don't want a penny from him. I want exactly what I came in with. But I know he won't go to a marriage counselor or a psychologist. I think he's depressed. One day he's up, one day he's down. The other day, he just broke down in tears on the subway. Can you believe that, a big man like him, crying like a baby all the way home?

D: Why did he start crying?

P: I don't know why, he wouldn't tell me. But this is the second time it's happened. The first time we were at a party, and as usual, he got drunk. He was arguing with this puny guy and he punched the guy in the eye. It became this big scene. He was lucky the guy didn't press charges, because the guy needed 13 stitches. Then when he got in the car, he started crying, really wailing. But it wasn't because he punched the guy.

The next day, when he was sober, and realized he could be in jail, or sued or lose his friend who threw the party, then he was sorry. But he didn't even call his friend, the host of the party, to apologize! I had to do it!

I think he feels powerless and that's why he's acting out: His job forced him to move to New York and he hates the City *and* his job. He's 30 years old and his mother still tells him what to do. Every time he comes home with an argument against me, he's always just come from visiting his mother. He's drinking more and more, I know he's drinking more to forget Montana and the space and more independent life he had there. And I know he's drinking to dull the pain of recently losing his father. He won't talk to me about that either. He goes to strip clubs so he can be around women who obey him—women who don't talk if he doesn't want them to—women he can control with his money. And now he wants to work part-time as a bouncer at his friend's nightclub, just so that they can beat up people occasionally, like he and his friend used to do when they were bouncers at that club in Montana. It's not like we need the money. He just wants all the girls there to rub up next to him and all the people there to look up to him, and say how cool he is for being this big handsome guy—and that's it—sex and violence and ego stroking.

D: And don't threaten my self-image. . . . I forgot that he's a Taurus. They always keep things inside until it hits threshold. Then they explode. . . . I don't know, maybe you're right: maybe the bouncer thing *is* a link to when he felt more powerful, more autonomous, had more control in his life. Maybe being violent, handsome and big are the three things he's always had and the only things he feels that he has left to hold on to?

P: What about me? When did I disappear? . . . [A minute passes as tears slide down her cheeks.] When were dating, and we broke up that second time, he followed me, he showed up at my job, he showed up at my house. And I'm sure if I leave him, he'll do that again.

D: Then, when you hit him with the divorce papers, you'll also serve him with a restraining order, so if he comes within 30 feet of you, he *will* be arrested.

P: It's not that easy in real life, little brother. Before—

D: Actually, it is that easy, and I will arrange it! But you must be 200 percent committed to not having in him in your life when he tries to worm his way back in, or intimidate you in to going back with him. Before, he didn't get the message strongly enough. Now, the cops will deliver the message—and he can think about it in jail.

P: Are the cops going to be outside of my office? No!

D: No, but he will be arrested. Let me look into these things and I'll call you back.

P: You won't do anything. You can't even help yourself. You've been out of school eight years and you've never had a permanent job.

D: That's not true. I'll be home for the rest of the night, so whatever time you want to call, call. This will end, and it will end before the New Year.

P: Yeah, you've always been very good at talking.

D: Later.

P: I know you're not going to help me with this.

D: Everything is going to be OK, you'll see, bye.

The next day, Paula calls David.

P: Hi.

D: Hey.

P: How are you?

D: Cool. How are you? What's up?

P: Not much. I just wanted to apologize for being cruel to you yesterday. I know you—

D: Forget it. I have some numbers for you. This is a help hotline for women in abusive situations, 800-621-HOPE. I didn't know that every 12 seconds a woman is battered, or that it usually starts with pushing and shoving or occasionally, like twice a year, before escalating to harder hits and more frequent beatings.

P: Yes, I know that.

D: This is a number to answer your questions regarding the divorce process and getting a free or inexpensive lawyer if he is going to challenge the divorce, which is the only case where you would need a lawyer. The counselor's name is Stacey and her direct dial is 212-577-3220; she's with the Victims' Services Domestic Law Project . . . If you do need a lawyer, you can also check with the American Bar Association or ask your psychologist for a referral, then compare notes and choose the best one. I'm sorry if I'm being didactic. This thing just has me really pissed off.

Anyway, your husband may contest the divorce on the grounds that there were less than "three examples of cruel or inhuman treatment over the last five years." I'm going to do some more research on the cost of an attorney and get back to you.

To get a restraining order in Manhattan, you have to go to Family Court in Brooklyn and apply for one. You can get it the same day, and the police will serve it to him. The Court may have evening hours; So you may want to check on that, so you won't lose a day of work waiting around to see a judge. Before going to Family Court, you may want to imagine you're the judge and play devil's advocate.

Getting a restraining order depends on the type of judge you get. You should speak with a counselor in Family Court's Protective Services Department before applying for one. Their counselors will help you strengthen your case for the order of protection. Be prepared to bring what evidence you have—pictures, police reports, threatening voice mail messages, whatever you have. Restraining orders usually run from 2 months to 12 months, depending on the severity of the case and the judge's discretion. When you get one, you may want to tell your manager and security, so if they see him outside, they can call the police—and he *will* be arrested. Even if he calls you, he *will* be arrested. Let me know if there's anything else I can do. I know this will be a big step for you if you decide to take it. [Jokingly] And I know you're a typical Cancer—you move as slow as a crab.

P: I don't have the income to survive on my own right now, but I will next year. But I just want to be sure I'm doing the right thing. So maybe I'll try to wait it out until then, see how it goes, if things dramatically change, I'll stick it out, but somehow I doubt they will. And I know you don't care about this, but I am a Catholic, and I do believe in the Catholic religion. So I really have to think about this and see a priest as well. But thank you, thank you for talking to me, thank you for checking into all this stuff. . . .

D: No thanks necessary. You're my sister. I would kill for you. . . . I'm sure you'll do what's best and everything will work out in the end.

P: Thank you for believing in me, David.

D: You've always been the rock in this family, the role model, so if I can reciprocate in anyway, my debt will never be repaid. I know you've walked through fire so I could live like I was to the manor born. And I know you've always felt talk was cheap, so I'm sure you'll handle.

P: I know in my heart that there's no romance, no communication, no shared values...and on his part, no compromise and no sacrifice. Sometimes I literally feel like a prisoner. But there is violence—so what's the point.

D: Here's the number for a highly recommended marriage counselor in the City; she works on a sliding scale. Maybe you should speak with her before you do anything. . . . When you go to shrinkage, you may want to ask her if your husband could have guilt about his father's death and if that guilt might explain some of his behavior. You know he never went to the hospital to visit his father. Maybe he feels guilty now that his father's passed, and he's torn up inside; maybe he feels that he can't talk to you about it because as a woman and a daughter, you wouldn't understand or wouldn't care, because all you seem to care about are petty things, like him being a slob. I don't know. . . .

But call me anytime—this has got me so confused, too.

P: You?

D: Yeah, we both don't know what to do—but I'll be damned if I stand by and see you be disrespected. I'll get a second job if it means you won't be in this situation, Paula.

Maybe it won't be the right thing to do, but I can't watch you stay in a relationship where you're beaten! Maybe for you to leave him, it'll take a knight in shining armor to step in and offer you a stronger relationship. I don't know. Whatever the case, I know you'll pray on it and your faith will give you the courage to steal back your heart. Just remember, if you need me, I will be here for you, anytime, OK?

P: [relieved, but depressed] OK. . . . I'm so glad I have you. Since Mom and Dad died it's been just us. And I'd feel so alone if I didn't have you. I'm sorry I burden you. . . .

D: No burden, big sis: [mock singing of the classic sibling song in high falsetto] *You ain't heavy, you're my sister.*

P: [Laughs slightly]

D: [Serious, hoping she will take the biggest risk of her life and move out]
I love you, Paula . . . Call me whenever, all right? If you need me in the middle of the night, I'm there!

P: [Fearful of a surprise attack from her husband at any time if she moves out. Unsure what her bosses would say or how they would react to her obtaining a restraining order. What would that information do to her corporate career as a marketing executive? Would her colleagues consider her working-class trash? How could she ever move into a shelter? They're so run down and unclean. What would she do with all her stuff?] . . . I love you too, David.

D: It'll be OK. You'll see. I prayed about it, and my God said you're going to be just fine. And He's never been wrong when we've requested his help, right?

P: That *was* miraculous! [Laughing at the memory of her asking David to ask his God, Ra, to quickly find them a parking space in congested mid-Manhattan traffic, after they had been driving endlessly looking for one. David's God had told him to look quickly to his right, and then in a second there it was—a spot next to Central Park, just big enough for her car. David then mockingly repeated the line from the movie *The Ten Commandments*: "Where is your God now, Moses!"]

D: Exactly. So call me tomorrow, OK?

P: OK.

[David switches to the Discovery Channel. A Himli woman stands on a mountaintop in Nepal in the half-light before dawn. She is in profile. A white lambskin cloak covers her face and head. She spins wool onto a spindle. David turns back on his movie. Catherine Deneuve and her lover are splashing bubbles at each other in the tub. David continues watching, half-titillated. Meanwhile, on the Discovery channel, a voiceover starts as the woman spins: This is Boria Sax for *Parabola* magazine here in Nepal. The subject of this month's episode is Fate and Fortune. It's been said that sometimes everything hangs by a single thread. In Greco-Roman mythology, destiny is controlled by the three Moirai, or Fates, who spin, measure out, and cut a thread for every human being. The act of spinning follows a cosmic rhythm, the spindle revolving like the alteration of day and night. The Old German word for "fate" is "wurt," which means "spindle." The thread of life emerges from the spindle as much as temporal events emerge from the eternal order. Similarly, the spider, relentlessly catching insects in its web, is also an image of fate. Our word "spider" derives from the Old English "spinthron," and it originally means the "spinner." Not only the Fates, but also many archaic mother goddesses, such as the Egyptian Neith, have been associated with spiders. The legends of many peoples, such as the Navajo and Hopi, tell that women first learned spinning from a spider deity.

The early Christian philosopher Boethius wrote of God turning "heaven like a spindle." Iconic pictures of a woman with a spindle were used to introduce representations of the zodiac in medieval art. The Virgin Mary was sometimes painted spinning as the angel came to announce that she would conceive the Son of God. It is almost as though her spindle had called forth the entire story of the Incarnation, Crucifixion and Resurrection.

Spinning has always been the most feminine of arts, in part because creation through spinning also resembles birth. The strand that emerges from a spindle suggests an umbilical cord. A caterpillar spins to create a cocoon, from which it is reborn as a butterfly. Spinning as a symbol of transformation appears frequently in European fairy tales, which are about coming of age, such as "Sleeping Beauty," which centers on the perilous transition from the timelessness of childhood to adulthood. In the tale, the princess slumbers for a hundred years as the result of a spindle. The period of sleep acts as a protective cocoon, a sheltered world in which the young woman can delay the choices of adulthood until she is ready. The tale was popular during the early industrial world, when it also expressed a longing to escape modernity into a kingdom that time had left behind.

Until the Middle Ages, the hand spindle, like the needle, was one of the very few tools in common use that had remained virtually unchanged since prehistoric times. The spinning wheel was probably invented in India and came into use in Europe during the last decades of the thirteenth century. It gradually took over not only the task of spinning but also the symbolic meaning of the older implement. It was faster and more easily adjusted, while suggesting an image of fate that was less harsh in its finality.

The metaphor of the spinning axis of fate suggested the popular allegory of the "Wheel of Fortune," which is one of the cards of the tarot. The goddess Fortuna turned a wheel, while figures representing different estates clung desperately to its rim. Though Fortuna held a cornucopia, a symbol of plenty, there was often a blindfold on her eyes. The topmost figure on the wheel wore a crown, while the one at the bottom fell into oblivion. The image expressed the aspiration and terror that men and women felt on the threshold of the modern world.

Today, the "Wheel of Fortune," has become the name of an immensely popular game show—a play on the word "fortune," which originally meant luck or chance but now more frequently means "wealth." We have reversed the meaning of the turning wheel: instead of calling for stoic acceptance, it has become a celebration of desire; instead of an expression of fate; it has become a game of chance. Similarly, the appeal of lotteries is the opportunity they present to place oneself at the mercy of the great unknown.

The "American Dream" is an attempt to cast off the past and make a new beginning, to liberate oneself from destiny. No longer born to a social class, a profession or even a religion, a person may change these many times during his or her life. Yet who or what is the self that has this power? Emptied of attributes, the individual is also deprived of autonomy and control. We have come full circle, and as our countless machines are integrated into an enormous network through computers, we return to the most archaic image of destiny—the spider moving along the "World Wide Web." The spider is a predator, a symbol not only of creation but also of death—an image that expresses both our fear and wonder as we move into the future.

As we proceed or progress, are we blind to fate or do we have blinders on? The three Fates mentioned earlier in the broadcast all share one eye. Like the Fates, do we only glimpse what is really happening, and as a result misunderstand what Jung called "synchronicity"? When we catch on, we learn to pay attention to "meaningless" irregularities and, instead, read them as signs, omens, and portents. This brings greater respect for the enigma of life. Heraclitus reminds us to read fate as character—we will be who we are if we are true to ourselves. As a word, *character* originally had to do with the craft of engraving a sign onto a stone, as can be found in Egypt's 5,000 year-old temples. Because our character bears out our fate onto life like a stamp, we invariably turn to story, as Laura Simms says, to glimpse its form. . . ."

At the end of David's movie, Catherine Deneuve is living in a rustic French chalet in the snow-covered countryside, with her female lover, who is lying on the couch reading as the fire roars. Catherine is lying on top of her, with her back to her, also reading. A blanket is draped over them. Credits roll. Months in real life pass. Spring comes. The weather is unseasonably hot. David tries to reach Paula, but she has taken a month-long leave of absence from her job. She is no longer at her old address. He is going crazy because he cannot find her. He thinks the worst. He can't sleep. Her e-mail address has been cancelled. She has vanished.

All of her friends are certain she will turn up, but he is the only one that knows the behind-the-scenes drama. All of them search but none of them are lucky. Paula is a very private person and she had told only him about her failed marriage and the physical abuse. Paula's husband has also vanished, or so it seems, for David has been unable to find him, although he has searched endlessly for both of them. He thinks he will have to hire a private investigator because the police are useless. He picks up the phone to again call the police about his missing person's report when he hears Paula's voice.]

P: How did you know to pick up?

D: My clairvoyance. It comes in and out. [Restraining his furious anger at her for sounding casual.] Actually, I was just about to call the police for the 15th billion time to ask them if they could help me out with a little problem.

P: [She pauses, considering what to say to heal him. She will not apologize. She does not apologize, to anyone.] I had to move out. He tracked me down. I lost most of my stuff. I had to move to a second place. I got a divorce. I eventually had to get that restraining order.

D: Did he hurt you?

P: No.

D: Are you OK? I was so worried about you, Peanut. Please don't ever do that again, baby. I really love you and care about you.

P: I know. And I feel the same way about you. I'm, OK, really. Everything is OK now.

D: I think I should find him and kill him!

[Silence]

D: [Trying to be compassionate] Did he contest the divorce?

P: I don't want to talk about it.

D: [At least not yet, he thinks of the girl born under the sign of cancer: She is slow to anything of personal importance] You could have stayed with me. [He is hurt that she did not do this.]

P: I'm an independent woman, David! I had to do it on my own!

D: Did he hurt you?

P: No.

D: [He is not sure if he believes this. He vows to find her ex-husband and cripple him if he did. Maybe he will find him anyway. Something he should have done long ago. Maybe he will leave him to the universe. David chooses to decide later about her ex's fate, when he is less emotional. Right now, he could punch a brick wall. He keeps telling himself that the important thing now is that she says she is OK. He tries to calm his anger at both of them.] How is the place where you are now? Is it safe?

P: Yes. I'm in an apartment now. And I'm looking at houses in Connecticut! [She is upbeat about this bit of news] Do you want to take the drive with me tomorrow to see the one I like?

D: I'd like to see you tonight.

P: You know I wouldn't have called you if I wasn't all right.

D: Hmmm…cool. [He is angry. He can't believe his sister and yet he can believe her. This is the way she operates. This is her character.] You may want to call your friends. They've been a little worried about you.

P: I will call them, but I wanted to call you first.

D: What time tomorrow?

P: I'll pick you up at seven on Saturday. OK?

D: I'll make some fried chicken.

P: Really? Great! I love your fried chicken! Does that mean we're having a picnic at that museum I like?

D: Boy, you're quick.

P: (smiling) Great.

D: The 'burbs, huh?

P: Yeah. You'll see: some of the houses are really cute, with lots of land.

D: I know you like that.

P: Yeah, peace and quiet…and nature.

D: [He sighs] So fall by Saturday morning and we'll roll.

P: OK. . . . Thank you, David.

D: No thanks necessary. I did nothing.

P: Actually, you did a lot.

D: I'm going to rent a fly whip for the trip.

P: [Laughs] A what?

D: A Porsche.

P: [Skeptical] If you must. But I'm driving.

D: Only after the Bridge. I've seen you drive in the City.

P: [Chuckles] Me???

D: It's nice to hear you laugh again.

P: [Smiling] See you Saturday.

D: [Incredibly relieved and thankful] Bye.

P: [Lovingly] Bye.

For Luz ("Light" in Spanish)

PROSE

3...I & I

Now I'm in this van. . . .

DON'T!

All I want is my money; the cash Shakim owes me. Loaned him a C over the summer cuz we'z boys back in the day—or else I wouldn't a loaned him shit. He's working the slopes for Jus, using too. But he hooked me last semester when I was short for books, so I said, "Okay, Shak, I'll put you D." But now financial aid said the loan I was supposed to get—I ain't getting. Counselor said shit's more "stringent." So now I need all my money.

"Don't worry 'bout it homeboy. Meet me up on the Boulevard at 4 o'clock, CCNY is on me. . . ."

5 o'clock came and the boy wasn't nowhere near Adam Clayton Powell! More like Malcom X.

DON'T NOBODY!

So I cut through a couple of lots, jet into the burnt out building, climb the rickety stairs, and knock on 2B's sheet metal door.
"Yo, Shakim, it's me!"

The door opens. Him and his boys scaling serious snow on the triple beam. House beats pumping. One light bulb dangling from the chipped ceiling. Everybody talking 'bout "getting paid in full, paid in full." He's trying to get me to chill, but I'm not wit it: "Yo, Shak, just hook me so I can break."

DON'T—DON'T NOBODY MOVE!

German Shepherds on our ass. Shotguns pumped. .45s aimed. No time to think twice. Cuffs crunch, lock, rip into skin. A tear streams down my face, mixing with the dirt and gravel I'm trying to spit out the side of my mouth. The Beast's forearm on my neck, flashlight in my eye. My wallet opened, pressed against my face.

"You Owen Chandler?"

"Yeah!"

"You're going to have a lot of time to study now."

Caught the Rodney King beat down on the way to the station for no other reasons than the obvious.

Now I'm in this van. . . .

No light. No ventilation. Can't hardly breathe from the smell of sweat and anger. Babylon production in full effect, a Neo-Middle Passage constructed by the Beast. Rough riding to Brooklyn, borough of kings, 20 of us—shackled, arms, legs, chain-gang style. Trying to remember how to breathe, how to jailhouse box, how to roll a winning combo for celo—is it 4-5-6? Damn! I need all my knowledge from the University of the Streets. *"I'm sorry, there's less money this year. Don't you have family or relatives you can borrow the money from? . . . Guidelines are more stringent this year. . . ."*

Chill, I and I . . . seen all a that: False concern manifesting existentially. Unviable options from casa blanca colonizers. *Ronnie, the Sequel,* cold rockin' the Establishment's collegiate version of the IRS. Voodoo Poppy called it. Education of the oppressed, take one, take two, take ad infinitum. For real this time . . . again. Bet—I and I, speak, seen, to me, all a that—word. Alchemizing foundations of tinsel and bad luck like Drew and transfusions. EZ, my knowledge, myself . . . I and I . . . through the eye of the needle . . . can still see Medina, whole. Cuz this is Maasai from the Nile . . . just in wrong place, wrong time, not destiny. . . .

I and I . . . seen all a that.

Down. . .for weeks, days, hours. . .
Big C.O. brother shouted outside my cell, "Chandler! You made bail!"

He grinned, like you lucky son-of-a-bitch.

I got in his grill, "What?!" Grabbed my nuts, like fuck you!

His grin broadened as he crunched his knuckles in his fist: "You'll be back."

I calmed down, got my cool back, looked him up and down like wasn't shit: "The first ones Nat Turner killed were the nigga overseers, right?" I laughed. Stepped. "Read about my case, baby boy! It's going to be in all the papers!"

I had told her not to do it, but she put all the money Columbia University had given her on the table. *Not my prince! Not my king!* She hugged me vice tight, whispered three words, which I echoed, and echoed again years later, after we had sued NYPD, again years later, after the dawn broke on our honeymoon villa overlooking Italy's glorious sun-splashed Amalfi Coastline.

Yeah, I and I seen all a that.

PROSE

6...The Lion's Heart

When I picked up the phone in my Harlem brownstone, I thought it might be my Dad. I'd have to kid him about the "preacher" Holyfield beating the "bully" Tyson in their championship fight that had just ended. He'd bet on the ex-heavyweight champ, "Iron Mike." My father loves boxing. When I was a kid we'd always watch the fights. He also liked to watch nature shows, reruns of *All in the Family* and *Home Improvement*. The only other thing he likes to watch now is *Oprah*.

I remember one episode of *Home Improvement* where the star's never-seen neighbor gives him some friendly advice: "When mother-in-law visit," he says in the stereotypical baritone of a Native American chief," man stay in garage! This universal law!"

I. The 400 Yo's

On an episode of what you might call *Home Improvement for Postmodernists* (the italicized title in German), with the Freudian quote below it: "What the children are up to." My Dad and I repaved our family's 100-foot driveway one July afternoon many years ago. We had just finished paving the backyard of our new fixer-upper: a three-family in freshly integrated East Flatbush, Brooklyn (read: white flight imminent).

On this torrid afternoon, our block looked like the intro to *The Wonder Years* TV show, but in various hues of black: African-American and Caribbean-American kids played football, catch, tag, you name it. And because of the holiday, firecrackers, M-80s and bottle-rockets fizzed, popped and boomed intermittently from every direction.

My father's stocky, powerfully built frame glided a steel trowel over the wet cement mix in slow figure eights.

"Naah," he growled, in a thick Jamaican accent, only half joking about my visiting grandmother. Sweat drops fell from his deeply creased, 45-year-old face. His square-jaw shook back and forth.

"Naah," he repeated, and then again, but almost in a whisper, "Naah," his voice cracking at the end. "She don't like me." He paused, rested his palms on his knees, took a deep breath, took a deeper breath that billowed his upper body. He sighed deeply as he let out a gust of air that sounded more like a groan. Then he shouted: "Because me black!"

Roy had wanted to conceal this anger and hurt from his son, who also looked maduro. Roy had tried hard to please his wife, but he would never be able to do so completely. Now the tension in the house had boiled over and booted him out to this project. His moist malt eyes held back the strongest and most paralyzing of fears: rejection. He said, more calmly: "She no like anybody that don't look like her." He continued troweling. A tear splashed to the wet cement. He smoothed it over.

My grandmother lives in Middlesex, London, a middle-class burg, with her retired, civil-servant husband who, like her, is partially Chinese, Irish and African. She's quiet, reserved, matronly. She looks like ex-Secretary of State Colin Powell's mother/*Mrs. Doubtfire*. She visited us for two weeks annually, and said little to my father each visit. Roy is a welding foreman and former competitive body-builder. She tolerated his presence in his own house the same way one awaits a sulfuric breeze.

Later, my father's words echoed in my head each time I looked at my grandmother. Up until this afternoon I had loved her. My grandmother didn't understand that demeaning darker blacks was actually self-hating and just as detrimental to lighter-skinned blacks. Questions blurred in my mind: "Aren't we all 'black'? Isn't it stupid to discriminate, especially in one's own *race*?" I despised the word *race*. I surmised that there must be white people and other people of color who are not racist because, if nothing else, medical researchers had already found that the majority of white Americans have some "black" blood. And according to author Salman Rushdie, when you hold down one thing, you hold down the adjoining.

Meanwhile, the top one percent of the nation, who control 90 percent of the wealth, laugh all the way to the bank at the middle-class and poor racist robots who uncritically execute their proclivities, right? The middle-class idiots and the poor robots don't realize that we all share the same fate, and that we have more in common than the I percent want us to believe. That's why MLK was killed. He was starting a poor people's movement that united the races. As always in America, it's about 1) who has the numbers on their side, and 2) who controls the masses and the technology (from the Winchester to the Internet) and 3) economic class (not real class, which is forthright honesty, discretion, dignity, compassion, sensitivity to others, and the courage to stand up for what's right—even if is unpopular and means you may be physically harmed).

It's never been about the artificial construct *race*. Just look at how much poor Southern blacks and whites have in common, and why they were, and continue to be, separated. It was where MLK was taking his unity movement before he was assassinated.

One night, "Grandmama" (I say this in a snooty mocking tone) came into my sliver of a room, accompanied on the nickle-tour of our newly renovated house by my mother, who showed her the collection of posters she'd purchased for me at Brooklyn's Kings Plaza Mall.

"Oh, yes, good," my grandmother said. "I know her."

My mother liked to surprise me with posters from her shopping sprees at Kings Plaza: The person on the door-length poster my grandmother recognized, a poster erected as ordered—and thus keeping all of the porn snugly within the advertising continuum—-was of an open armed and puckered Marilyn Monroe in fishnets and bustier. Joining her (left to right on my walls) were: blond model Cheryl Tiegs, tan and wet in the Pacific surf wearing a string bikini; and Angel Farrah Fawcett, showing a little cleavage and smiling broadly as she twirls as a big blonde curl. Every time my mother bought me home a new poster I was always like, "Whatever." The poster collection cracked my friends up ("Yo, can she hook you up with at least a token sister? A little Pam Grier for a brother, something, just a little affirmative action." Then they'd all bust a gut laughing). None of us paid attention to the girls on my wall. My mother didn't know that Denise Nicholas was the reason to watch *Room 222*, nor how many times I watched Pam Grier apply lotion to her legs in *Buck Town*.

My parents told me when I was 15 that they thought I was gay, so I guess in retrospect that they were trying to steer me in the right direction. This they didn't have to tell me: they were the type of black people that were so mentally oppressed that they felt "white is right." When my parents explained their conclusion about my sexual orientation to me, I thought, God how little you know me. As fate would have it, I had spent the better part of that afternoon down in my basement having torrid sex with the captain of the cheerleaders. God, she was cool, but I digress. When my parents expressed their fear to me I could only smile inside while remembering Debbie's perfect pom poms and what I did with them. Outwardly, I tried to look very serious and not bust out laughing. Sure, I thought to myself, think whatever you want to think of me. I could give a fuck. Jump to whatever conclusions you want to jump to because I don't bring any girls home when you're around or have them call when you're here. I would never inflict your ignorance on any of my lovely angels, and oh, yes, they're all black and beautiful.

These poster gifts, manifestations of my mother's learned values from post-colonial Jamaica, were not to be respectfully declined. My two older sisters viewed the posters like exotic-zoo-animals. "Mom went to Kings Plaza again, huh?" they'd say as they scanned the latest poster. They'd look the posters up and down, then shake their heads, not understanding my mother's standard of female beauty. When my sisters looked at the posters they recognized their privileged rivals for Mr. Right and developed what would become a lifelong dislike and distrust of The Blonde.

My mother disliked all things "tacky and niggerish." However, she did discover white-trash girlfriends, who were aging club sluts. She decided to make their families part of our lives. On weekends, our house morphed into Michael Jackson's ghoulish "Thriller" video as her girlfriends prepared to paint the town, and their faces, red. My father shared my mother's fondness for bottom feeding, and soon befriended a drifter (think uber-square Kyle MacLachlan—Charlotte's momma's boy husband from *Sex and the City*—trying to play a Hell's Angel type). Dad rented the drifter a room in our house and found him a job at his plant—only to have homeboy become obsessed with the occult and have a 9II freakout several months later.

I had noticed the early warning signs when I had to play Toni Morrison's Macon Dead by going to the drifter's room to collect the rent, e.g., the purple pentagon star painted on the linoleum floor, which was surrounded by books on Satanic rituals and related matter. Before flipping out, the drifter eventually repainted the white walls and ceiling, red and black, respectively. For a moment, I thought he was getting down with the Black Power movement.

My parents' racial mandate regarding friendships meant my friends from the projects who were, for lack of a better word, homicidal, had to go because they were definitely niggers; my friends from the projects who were not homicidal also had to go because they were still niggerish—"Get rid of them." I reminded my parents that my friends were OK by me. I refused to discard my "*homies*," and refused to join an all-white Boy Scout troop miles away in a neighborhood where some of the residents like to go "coon hunting" with baseball bats. For refusing to join this troop that had more in common with the drinking habits of the 4077 M.A.S.H. than the imagination of Norman Rockwell, my Dad assigned me hard labor, orchestrated to the tune of the lash, "From can't see in the morning, 'till can't see at night," as Malcom X used to say. Imagine those art-house black and white photos of toiling Mississippi chain gang workers, with the fat guard and his snarling, leaping Doberman straining the metal "choker" chain, drool hanging from its mouth as the inmates worked. The dog for us was Tarzan, our white German Shepherd/Husky, and she was junkyard mad. My father would yell at me, "You lazy ras!" and then tell her, "Attack!"—as if she needed prodding—and unleash her from the chain that gored a necklace of red dots around her dirty white-fur throat. What masculine ideals was this supposed to teach me? Was this supposed to engender my toughness? Or was this a lop-sided game affirming his status as omnipotent ruler of the household? Was this his freedom and pleasure, as when he would beat my naked bare ass? Whatever the case, I took my scars and learned to literally kick that dog's ass.

My brother, however, joined the boy-scout troop and came back enthusiastically chanting one of their songs: "I want to be an Airborne Ranger! I want to live a life of danger! I want to go to Vi-et-nam! I want to kill some Vi-et Cong! Sound off, 1, 2, 3, 4—1-2-3-4!" My brother happily recounted the racist jokes the scoutmaster had told him. He thought they were funny. My bother did not make friends with guys in the projects. He first feared them and then went to war against them. They gave him a couple of deep scars: one on his face and one on his leg. One afternoon I came back to the projects to find what seemed like the whole upper terrace chasing him back to our building. I was holding back the door as best I could so he could get in the elevator. When neighbors came out of their apartments to see what all the fuss was about, they ran, figuring they'd get him later. My brother learned to use the word *niggers* a lot, and until he was in his late 30s, he never realized that his white friends who went "coon hunting" would also hunt him.

But I digress. I was telling you about my dad. My father knew that his mother-in-law disliked him, but he did not think my mother would be the one to hurt him. My father's self-evasion from his African roots had come back to him that summer holiday afternoon. It returned as a vicious counter-puncher, pummeling his face into agony with each succeeding revelation.

First, his wife's loathing of things low and dark was form and function of their marriage. Second, he would never have his wife's total respect because he would never be white nor light. Third, he would never be fully "American" because he would always, ultimately, be from Kemet. Fourth, he would never be able to afford the "price of the ticket" for U.S. citizenship because it required an application of racism that would render him insane. This lifted veil, Dubois's duality of consciousness and a spinning prism of hatred, caused bitter tears of anger, resentment and unrequited love, both of self—and of his wife's. This new-found knowledge rocked my father to the core of is manhood, and he fell to his knees. The lion in winter.

Before his roar would die, he would learn that virtue alone earns total respect, and such virtue is not the sole province of any "race" or culture. There are niggers in every culture. Yet virtue is a hallmark of real "class." (Honesty, discretion, dignity, compassion, sensitivity to others, and the courage to stand up for what's right—even when it is unpopular and when it means you may be physically harmed. That is class, as I see it.)

My father could not admit this universal law regarding virtue, nor that my mother's thinking was self-defeating and self-hating. Doing so would have confirmed a complicity in the hatred of his peers, and consequently, shatter the image he held of himself as innocent and good.

My Dad, a gregarious individual, the man for whom the phrase "a people person" was invented, naively believed in each person's goodness and honesty, which led many of his friends and family to take advantage of him. Prior to that pyrotechnic July afternoon, he had never uttered a word about racism. As with most families, his silence mirrored his mate's. Hot-button issues, like my grandmother's self-hatred and envy of whites, were never discussed. There were to be no questions regarding sex, his '40s-style chauvinism, or the leaves of mental illness on both sides of our family tree.

Curiously, my four siblings and I were encouraged to discuss current events and the fine arts in polite fashion at the dinner table, but never police officers shooting kids of color in the back of the head. If you called either of my parents a whore, or worse, for disowning their out-of-wedlock children and leaving them behind in sunny Jamaica like forgotten breadfruit—you might as well report a homicide.

I could never tell my parents that my step-brother had sexually assaulted me when I was 9 and maybe that is why they thought I was gay. That would be a futile discussion.

My mother's favorite painter was the womanizer Picasso, who she likened to the Cuban dictator Castro. And she likened Fidel to my father. After a long day of shopping, she would come in and conspiratorially ask my sisters and I, "Where's Castro?" She never said this to my father, who she would never leave, because "all Jamaican men are alike," and she would never divorce him, because she could wind up with a Jamaican man who's worse, and how could she support four kids by herself. She feared Castro as she loved him. Although I knew a variety of Jamaican men, I understood her fears; as well as her one unspoken fear: she did not want to live without a man.

When my brother, the eldest, heard her explanations for not leaving my father, I could see from his ebony face that he did not feel good about himself. He was deeply concerned about our mother's safety, and one night many years later he would come between my parents as my father attempted to strike her down.

My parents' silence on sensitive matters like race and sex kept their identities whole and clean (they had grown up dirt poor in Jamaica after being abandoned by their fathers). My mother, who was a smart girl who excelled at math, had walked more than 20 miles from "country" to "town" to see her biological, who was a successful local businessman with five kids and a stellar reputation as a pillar of Jamaican society. He told my mother flatly that there was nothing he could or would do for her. "You're nothing to me." I imagined my mother walking back on those desolate country roads and how those words must have echoed in her head, cut her to her core, fueled her self-hate and nurtured her dislike of men.

As mature adults, regardless of content of character, my parents shunned anyone who did not look and act respectable and mainstream, anyone who did not have strong moral values, a home (except if you were white, like the aforementioned drifter). They also did not like you if you did not have "good home training" (read: corporal punishment rooted in Jamaica's British colonial rule). You see, most of Jamaica is not the rastafarian-pot-smoking image sold to Americans by the tourist board. Most of Jamaica is conservative and drug-free. The government did not even like Bob Marley until they found that they could pimp his image to boost tourism. In Jamaica, there are the "bald heads" and the "rastas" and you know which camp Bob fell into. Accordingly, Bobus sang, "We got to chase those crazy bald heads outta the town."

My parents didn't question their own policy of exclusion or its origins; and they did not because of their perceptions of how American "niggers," "Ricans," and "Jews" dressed, walked, talked and smelled. Only when "the white man," as my parents liked to label racism, crashed the cement ceiling on their heads with stone-cold reality, did they vent. At those times, I would laugh to myself as they complained: now you feel me.

What then, did my father, by his silence and complicit actions, raise me to respect? The assumption in my father's tears that afternoon was that a black man was not worthy of life: he could not claim the dignity of manhood. He could not tell my mother, or her mother, that he would not tolerate any disrespect in his home. They had found his insecurity and worked it.

My father was forced to face his identity that day solely because it was menaced. When my grandmother visited, she made him a stranger to himself to his castle and to the identity that he had co-created, along with Jamaica ante-bellum rule. Under the coat of his faux strong character was a nakedness he was ashamed of, a naturalness he could not trust, a skin color to be clothed by debt-inducing conspicuous consumption: "I am just as good as anybody else. See, I have two cars, a big house, a nice lawn." *I am somebody!* to appropriate Jesse Jackson's presidential-campaign chant. What could be more American? The longest, smoothest driveway, the newest car, the best-looking lawn, and the biggest house on the block. Moral virtue had been sold for the power to consume.

Delivering this feeling of inadequacy was my grandmother's way of putting my father in his place, or what some might call, "keeping the nigger in check." But who, my father might have asked, will civilize the colonial British, or my Grandmama? My father's inability to show or voice his anger toward her the remainder of her fortnight was a direct result of hi Brit-ophile, colonial upbringing, still thriving among England's most ardent worshippers: many Americans.

My Dad's silence was in direct proportion to the relative impotence of the American identity and its envy of European culture. My grandmother knew this well. She also knew the truth. She had seen the identity of England's ruling class harassed after WW II, and watched as the snobbery of the wealthy was made to feel self-conscious, defensive, guilty. But she watched with pride as Americans fawned over Lady Di and Charles' wedding and early marriage. She knew my father prized my mother's light skin and what that skin represented Bed-Stuy to Brixton.

The only television program I had ever seen my mother watch—and she watched it from the edge of her seat—was "The wedding of the century": the spectacular fairytale wedding of Prince Charles and Lady Diana Spencer, a wedding that the poor of Britain financed with their taxes. In very messy American fashion, Charles and Di would, of course, later divorce. And later she would die in a horrible car crash, arguably for trying to marry a man of color.

And so, I knew that after repaving the driveway that afternoon, I would be "housed" (as my friends referred to a severe ass whipping) for whatever offense, small or large, real or imagined. I knew this as surely as I knew the source of my father's anger was an identity that controlled and suffocated him, specifically formed and pointedly utilized at the moment of lashing my bare flesh—as if I were a slave in a black exploitation film: Mandingo Part III, the Brooklyn Bondage. At that moment—railing at me to beg—my father was precisely executing the goals of the post-colonial government that had poorly educated him; thus accomplishing the aims of the rulers who had nurtured him. He was carrying out the goals of the vicious slave-owner for whom the term lynching owed its namesake.

But Willie Lynch's lessons of vicious beatings and heinous murder, all in the name of getting slaves to obey, now mentally tortured my Dad, at the same that he physically tortured me, screaming at me to beg as he lashed me. Willie Lynch had sought to use violence to instill fear and respect, to divide the black family and to conquer the black male. His goal was to have the black women and children watch wild horses pull apart disobedient black men so that they would be filled with fear, and have respect of the slave owner. My father was Willie Lynch's dream: the plant foreman-cum-neocolonial overseer. Paid to silence anyone at the plant (ation) or at home who was disobedient, "shiftless" or questioned his identity and authority. The paradigm of slavery had found a new home and displaced aggression was working overtime.

From the time I could speak, I had a quick tongue and a precocious wit. As I grew older, I had many ideas on how to more effectively and efficiently execute our nightly home-repair projects. Whenever my Dad had to adopt one of these ideas, he became enraged and beat me severly, ostensibly for some other petty reason. One day, while working on a home-repair project, I explained to him that I was committed to both family and work projects, but I could not be expected to give my all if I was not involved both mentally and physically. What was I thinking? This engendered even greater violence.

I learned to shut up and give the acceptable minimum, perhaps like the proverbial "lazy nigger." Yet the beatings/good home training continued on a daily basis, as if they were his pressure valve. My mother added to my father's verbal and physical daily assaults with her own displaced aggression, nightly verbal lashings about my dubious sexuality or lazy personality that met me each evening when she came home from work and/or school. Knowing that I was going to get a double or triple dose of hatred each day fucked me up because I couldn't understand what I had done to deserve it—every day—and I loved them with all my heart in spite of all the public humiliations, which were worse than the private beatings.

I would like to see how you would fare in this environment for 18 years. It was like they were trying to break me, break my spirit. But the black man cannot be broken. We were here first and we will be here last. They had silenced my mouth. For now. I determined that this would be a long-term game, and I would laugh last. Now, if they could only make me learn to beg.

The public humiliations led me to believe that this was how I was supposed to be treated by any and everyone—born to lose—since this is how the people who were supposed to love me and protect me treated me. Even then, I knew there were

those in worse situations, so I kept my head up and pushed sui-
cide and homicide thoughts far from me. It was all just a matter
of time. I was just doing a bid on Maggie's farm, as Britain's
working class said about working in Prime Minister's Margaret
Thatcher's London.

One summer Saturday, my Dad yanked my 9-year-old body
out of the shower by the neck, held me aloft, dragged me into the
living room, then beat me like a wet dog in the living room in
front of aghast, formerly cocktailing, guests and relatives. It was
a way for him to display his power. He also made it a priority to
beat me in front of my sisters' pretty girlfriends until I begged
for mercy. He would give me the words to say as he went off.
I could take the beating, but I didn't want the girls, who were
cringing in horror, to see anymore, so I said the words, albeit
without the required emotion. It was the lesser of two evils I
guess. Up until then, some of them had been interested in me.

"One day you're going to see that I raised you right," my
father declared one night at dinner when I was in my teens, rel-
ishing the last of his beer, then nodding in self-affirmation. The
ostensible goal of educating a son to the struggle of life through
direct verbal and physical challenges is one method of teaching
a young male that life is pain, and that a man must constantly
fight to earn and maintain the respect of others; And the item
most worth fighting for at this early stage of male development
is self-respect and self-hood. The person to be defeated for this
invaluable prize is usually the one who has had complete domin-
ion over your life. For example, the patriarch of TV's *The Cosby
Show* once said to his teenage son: "Boy, I brought you into this
world, and I can damn sure take you out!" The boy replied by
looking down—dejected, depressed and defeated.

My Grandmama watched my father give me some good-
home training from the window that July afternoon. She "tsked

tsked" to my mother, who had just returned from another day of heavy shopping. She complained about "the savage." My mother thought the good-home training to be excessive punishment on one hand. On the other, though, she had witnessed it in her own normal upbringing—and my father had promised to stop "housing" my sisters, so that was at least, as Martha Stewart would say, a good thing.

At that time, my Catholic guilt got the best of me. I thought then, *My father is right. I'm wrong. I'm disloyal. I'm betraying the one who loves and provides for me by questioning his logic.* Later, I learned that these thoughts were similar to the way my father felt he shouldn't question the injustice or inequality of his beloved America. Why question himself and the government that had given him this Jamesian opportunity for a life of liberty and the pursuit of happiness? Why shatter the assimilationist dream? Why shatter the illusion of being all in the family?

Yet, my father's power over me revealed not his strength, but his weakness. His attempts to silence me only compounded his frustrations. Decades of being unable to see and challenge the murky roots of his problems, find solutions and move forward, only resulted in continuing, albeit comforting, patterns of negative behavior.

The uneasy sense of self that is the undercurrent beneath my parents' personalities is not anchored. Nor can it be cleansed until it is critically examined. Only then will they know that their crucible is stained with the blood of my siblings. And that theirs is a ravenous identity based on the boldest and weakest of fictions: race. While their material well-being depends on adhering to these fallacies, they will never be able to assess their true histories nor accumulate true wealth, until they are free to take from that history what they need, and add the courage of their humanity.

As a small boy, I had feared never having my father's love. So I imitated my brother and became a "yes man"—praying that would work. In this training, I learned how to be silent and phony (those slowest of suicides). These actions became my hope, a hope that dies like a lion's heart.

But were my humanity and unformed manhood to be placed at the feet of my father's delusions? Was my spirit, and my will, to be broken and ground to dust like some slave's?! I lay on my fold-out bed that July 4th night giving the criss-crossing gullies on my back air, letting the blood dry, still feeling the after-burn of the lash, seething, thinking: I have proven I can endure this love—I have been too patient. It is time to change the power equation or time to jet.

II. The Power Equation: Disneyland and Diphtheria

Harlem: Subconsciously a place where everything is black. For the conscious mind, however, there are subjective news tropes of KFC-eatin' "welfare queens," alarming illiteracy, accelerating poverty and its notorious and vibrant offspring—child abuse—via "reforms," like the welfare bill, that starves single white mothers, potential militia recruits and less violent poor white males, like cartoonist R. Crumb's brother "Sir" Charles.

Those aforementioned white faces are grizzled, their emaciated bodies slump in freezing doorways of hamlets like Hell's Kitchen, aka Time Square, aka Disneyand East, a neighborhood once populated by poor Irish immigrants who roasted "mickies" (potatoes) over metal drums filled with burning wood and garbadge. Historically, it was a community where culture brought people together. Ironically, this area is now populated by new families and wealthy residents. Some of whom wish to live in harmony, not live together, as long as you are the "right kind" of neighbor. This burg is increasingly referred to by some as Clinton.

On another macro plane, the recent workplace transformation in New York City is as dramatic as the U.S. shift from liberalism (the 1970s) to conservatism (the 1980s and 1990s), or on a more micro level, it's the struggle Michael Milken went though with the changing of the guard in investment banking in the 1980s. Milken represented a more aggressive and less genteel (read: gentile) breed of bankers: the difference between the "haves" and the "gots." But Milken underestimated the importance of truth and decorum, as well as the gangsta in Old Money (lessons not lost on that lady-killer Claus von Bulow). The simultaneous right-wing attack on art funding, and controversial gay artists like Mapplethorpe in the late '80's and early '90s, pushed many open-minded New Yorkers with an appreciation for civility out of the City, and the country. Many of the new species in New York now appear to be from sheltered backgrounds (e.g., Daddy's small but profitable company, first ski chalet, etc.).

The distant horizon between both coasts appears to be a red desert between the "haves" and the "have-nots," sand colored by blood and a digital divide filled with extreme citizenship and numerous choices. For those tempered by the Gulf War, jolted by the Rodney King rebellions, savaged by the cuts to education, lied to by the Great Vacillator, appalled by the human bonfire at Waco, and the taint of conspiracy surrounding the Oklahoma City and WTC bombings, the separation grows wider every second.

For this period of American history: the birth of the new millennium, considered by some a second Reconstruction, the question is whether non-income generating white males, women and people of color—the majority of Americans in the new millennium—will "move toward greater coalition building based on their shared interests. . . . direct[ing] a lot of energy toward political and economic empowerment," to quote Yale historian John Blassingame. Or whether there will be renewed militancy to re-secure and advance such power, which is the view of Columbia University Reconstruction scholar Eric Foner. The percolating question in fin-de-siecle America was whether the wretched of the U.S. soil would become as wicked as the French peasantry of 1793: Would more racial explosions flare across the nation? Would more Oklahoma City-type bombings occur? Would the young's cool facade, so like the ocean's calm surface, show its discontent and rage like a hurricane in New Orleans? And would this anger create, as it has throughout history, and as it does now in Egypt, forge an opportunity for another type of fascism? Or would it create an altogether different type of peace?

The rulers will write the historical answer.

III. Karma: Back to the Essence

Six years later. Now working as an investment banking analyst on Wall Street after graduating from Brown University and Columbia's MBA program. I went to Wall Street to learn the skills necessary to start my own company and to get the checks necessary to pay back the enormous school loans hovering over my head. I had gone to Ivy League schools because as a black man I need everything working for me. I had learned early that regardless of a black man's profession or field, the margin for error is much slimmer. There is no room for mistakes. There are no second chances. The rules are different and that's just the way it is.

Although affirmative action has benefited white women and other people of color, including Asians, more than African-Americans (please read the actual law and check the stats, but like welfare, it's easier to dismantle if it has a black face), black men have to be better educated and twice as good as those we compete against, because, ironically, we are the beast in the unconscious hegemonic psyche. That's life in America. Unfair perhaps, but get over it.

One sub-zero February night in NYC, I purchased a new pair of Red Wing motorcycle boots in Times Square: the Tragic Kingdom, a vibrant theater of the absurd, an area surrounded by a storm of color and noise where tourists crane their necks to see heaven-high neon advertising, billboards of buxom blondes in bustiers, as they absent-mindedly bump into city residents, who, unlike the tourists, refuse to reward depressing street performers.

On this night, daredevil bike messengers blew viciously into their whistles, dangerously dipping between buses, pedestrians and endless lines of yellow cabs. Steel bands drummed thunderously as cars honked in competition with screaming police and fire sirens. The smell of vendors' hot dogs filled the air, complemented by the odors of coarse mustard, hot roasted peanuts, car exhaust and winter frost. At rush hour, I walked elbow-to-elbow with two pregnant photo assistants worrying aloud about child care costs and job security, Russian businessmen devaluing their bad press as sophistry from the "evil empire's media machine," and middle managers debating the pros and cons of the newest Chevy minivans. We all moved as one frigid, shuddering mass, pressing against the wind, shuffling forward, hugging our big coats tighter, and disappearing momentarily through veils of steam rising from the streets. . . .

A silver "A" train whooshed in like a bullet as my new boots, a bit loose, clomped down the subway steps. I blew on my hands and jumped on the "A." I was headed to bourgie Queens: Cambria Heights, the racial safe haven for '40s *Ebony* icons like Billie Holiday, Count Basie, and Louis Armstrong. I had to get some photos from my parents (at my girlfriend's request) and say goodbye, because there had been too much talk and no structural change. I had talked to my family about "my issues" concerning race, class, sex and culture. They had "yessed" me to death but did not change. They ridiculed me behind my back as a naïve idealist. I would have preferred a straight "no" rather than the covert ridicule. They did not want to debate many things, including how love factored into psychologist Franz Fanon's hypothesis that Black men marry white women for psychological uplift and Black women marry white men for income potential.

Family gatherings had become repeat performances of *Death of a Foreman*, co-starring the author as a 9-year-old sitting in the family's station wagon with the wood-side paneling, chewing blocks of grape Now & Laters candy while his Dad visited numbers joints, OTBs, and mistresses. I thought my father was hopeless as I chewed a fat grape wad of Now & Laters. And I knew from the way that he had thrown plates and glasses at my sisters' bare legs and blackened their eyes, that he was also a coward. During those times, my own inner-self felt only confusion: Why is this necessary? We're intelligent children, what is this supposed to teach us: My life as a child meant the same thing as it does for adults in America, "Shut up and do what you are told"? I read a Rushdie line somewhere: do not beat your children, life will do a good enough job.

For my father's twilight, a man living in the country that Ralph Waldo Emerson called "the asylum of all nations," there will be no American dream—-no wealth, no power, no true freedom. Only indebtedness to credit cards and my sister's (an IRS agent's) financial acumen and assistance. For all his "good nigger" work at the plant, he was given the proverbial crumbs when the plant closed in the financially austere early '90s. His goodness and servitude went unacknowledged. His allegiance unreciprocated. *But love that loyalty!* On a larger stage, it is what happened to the brutal Bokassa, the recently deceased, self-proclaimed "Emperor for Life" of Central African Republic, who was propped up ("jebbed" into office) by the French then disposed of by them when his services were no longer required. (As fate would have it, the black puppet he initially deposed replaced him. Karma.) When you hold down one thing you hold down the adjoining.

However, 24 years of watching the creamy middle twist off for the milky dunk had left me with voluminous notes. My mother had urged us to mock my father, "Castro," the former "playa," behind his back, because he would never make any "real" money. She resented him for not struggling to educate himself as she had, and for not striving to become a buppie (black urban professional). My father's education had extended to the fourth grade. My mother—who often liked to shake her fist and say she wished she'd been born a man—"Oh, the things I would do!"—became an insurance company executive (she had arrived in America with only a 10th grade education, the birth of affirmative action and an iron will). She had examined my first Wall Street check wide-eyed and made it clear that I earned more than my father ever would.

My father now felt like Caesar in his final days. His mother had abandoned him at birth for the bright lights and fast times of Spanish Town and Kingston, Jamaica. (My father had waited on his mother grudgingly in her ill, elderly life, and leapt with joy at her funeral.) He also knew that his mother-in-law hated the sight of his wheelbarrow gut, and the way his size 42 jeans slid to hip-hop half-mast. My grandmama felt her beauty-queen daughter could have done much better than this working-class pig.

Who would love, honor and obey my father? Who would be mute on command? Who would give him increased status and easy conquest in this cruel world?

One afternoon in my youth, I was surprised but not shocked that my 14-year-old brother discovered a stash of bizarre pornography in their bedroom. Why did my father turn to one of our nation's fastest growing industries—its revenues presently surpass book publishing, $4 billion, by $1 billion—an outlet allowing him to fantasize about having power over obscure objects of desire, an entertainment affording him the opportunity to control, use and dispose of unknown women's vulnerable bodies as often as new issues or movies appeared? Most people think of pornography as *Penthouse* and *Playboy*. But the vast majority of it is far uglier. Women of all colors are violated for entertainment, then exploited economically and spiritually.

Men want women to be sexy, but some of us don't understand (or care) that it's extremely difficult to be someone's private dancer with the numerous pressures of living in today's society, especially when you are the principal bread-winner for a family and the income gap between the genders has not closed since women entered the workforce. If I want women to be sexy, I must be sexy, stronger, a better listener and more romantic. I must create real and lasting opportunities for women to reach the highest echelons of every job and career—and not because I want them to be sexy—but because it's right, just, good for the country, and an excellent example for the free world, which we, as Americans, are the self-appointed leaders of.

Tirades about the laziness of American blacks and the adult movies he showed my brother and I when we were in our early teens in the basement was Roy's idea of Sex Ed. For my brother, it was the foundation for his liking his women "scantily clad and obedient," cheating on his wife, firmly believing "niggers always want something for nothing," hanging solely with white thugs as a teen, and wanting to be a Guiliani cop (my mother didn't want him to become a cop, but only because they have to take an oath to arrest any criminal, regardless of relation).

My brother refused to go to college, so my father made him join the armed forces. My brother chose to become a "dark green" Marine grunt, instead of a Navy officer, as my father had wished.

Sons define themselves and their success in life by their father's character and accomplishments. Fathers live their failed dreams through their sons (look at Tiger Woods living out his father's dreams). My father wished to be an actor or in the military. And who paid the price for his failure? The military's recent woes regarding sexual harassment (e.g., the infamous Tailhook conventions) speaks volumes about what is tolerated in that closed society. As one war writer put it, "When morals go down, morale goes up." In society at large, the problem is well illustrated by the Senate confirmation hearings for Supreme Court Justice Clarence Thomas. When his former employee, Anita Hill, charged that he had sexually harassed her, the due process and result of the hearings showed just how out of touch our elected leaders are—the majority of whom continue to be old, monied white males from our society's wealthiest one percent.

How does this translate in the workforce? *Fagetabout* the good fellas who distribute adult cinema to responsible legitimate cable corporations. A better question is why does the industry of Hugh Grant—a man once in love with a strong-willed woman, who may not always want to fellate the big movie star at his request—frequently depict women being raped, mutilated, etc.? Is it because of the perceived Darwinian threat: Destroy what you cannot control or it will destroy you? Control women and their bodies or they will inherit the Earth? They have the power to stop male life. In the high-grossing movie *The Godfather II*, the princely Don's WASP wife tells him she had an abortion without his knowledge, because she would never bring another male child into his violent world. The Don batters her in response. (*The Godfather* is a premier "boy movie" that provides a lesson to "good" girls about marrying below their class.)

Does such thinking co-exist with the idea that the hot babe can triumph in the struggle of might makes right by use of her sexual prowess to transform even the strongest of men into a fool for love? "Girlfriend, Samson is sprung!"

Do men lack that control, that strength? Are we a monolith?

My father's need to create a space where he is superior and can manage his identity and future through money, physical force and progeny transcends race and class. 50-year-old Wall Street law partners discreetly purchase *Juggs* and jelly beans on their lunch hour and later meet with women associates, whom they view as credible, competent and equal as men, right? Such actions also detract from the glass ceiling, the gulf of non- and miscommunication between the sexes, sexual harassment and the divorce ratio. The airbrushed, glossy marketing clashes with the reality of independent American women, who are more Roseanne than Pam.

I never rebelled against what I saw growing up, never despised my emerging arrogance, selfishness or passion to succeed at all costs—to hell with the ethics—regardless of loss of pride or dignity (I could easily have been a crass, phony talk-show host; small surprise that I wanted initially to be a journalist, a profession where there are no difficult licensing exams, only numerous extramarital affairs). Growing up, I lived only on my unquenchable thirst to survive the daily good-home training.

I & I

The day I decided to end the *Mandingo Tales*, when I was 14, my father and I were working in the back yard. I picked up a long 2x4 and introduced it to the side of his face with a swing that would have made batting champ Barry Bonds proud. My Dad spun like a top, fell and passed out. I learned the hard way that violence and money are the only things violent people respect. It is their only language. My mother, who no doubt heard the flush smacking of wood to skull, ran from the house yelling and screaming, sure her husband was dead. She knelt over his body crying, begging God to let him live. It was all so melodramatic. He didn't even fall into the ditch with the jagged slabs of concrete as I had intended. I just walked away. I had planned to jump into the ditch, pick up a 50-pound slab and thrust it onto his head—all the dog bites and injuries ran through my head as I swung the long 2x4. God saved him. My father eventually came to and staggered inside with my mother, like a wobbly football player helped off the field.

That was the end of the physical assaults but the start of increased verbal abuse. Eventually, I barked intelligence in his face that backed him up. He was stunned, as if he had heard me speak for the first time. He walked away. We had no honest communication after that. We had nothing.

In retrospect, I should not have stooped to his level. I should have called a trusted adult or a child abuse hotline, but I fleetingly thought that if those options failed, things might get fatally worse for me. Clearly, I didn't think through the consequences of my incorrect and violent action. I could easily be on death row now. I should have thought harder about a peaceful solution.

Now, years later, walking through the nice residential community of Cambria Heights, I liked the way the heavy motorcycle boots felt: sure, steady. . . The wind bit my face, making me shiver and my chin an icicle. The houses were all the same: attached, gingerbread colored, deceptively thin, with stamp-sized front lawns and brown wooden doors like closed, drawbridges. My mother opened the yawning door, stepping back from the blast of wind. She was plump, anxious. Her amber eyes steeled. "Come in!" she commanded. She didn't understand why I didn't want to be part of a family that was anti-black and consequently anti-human. I didn't want to hear any more promises for individual and family "shrinkage" that would never be followed up on. I didn't want to hear any more duplicitous words about our need to confront our self-hate. I didn't want to listen without love.

I didn't know where the money was, according to them. I didn't know how to play the game. I sat on the Victorian sofa and flipped through the photo albums. My mother's orange and white cat, Trixie, stopped lapping milk from a saucer. She came over and meowed a hello while rubbing her arched back against my leg. I rose and walked toward the petite, angry woman, with her "good hair" in a chignon. As I came toward her, I realized I didn't know her.

"Take care," I said, stuffing the photos in my backpack. I could never imagine the pain that had brought her here, to this person she had become.

Identity is a technicolor dreamcoat that beams rays that are harsh, cool or some variant in between, depending on the light hitting the mosaic of our personality? Or is it that innate pillar, that spirit or soul that shouts in the tempest? Or is it our critique and use of our nature and nurture? I walked toward the door confused. My boots echoed loudly, menacingly, on the in-laid oak floors. Sadness welled up in my chest and throat. I stopped and looked up the stairwell. I shouted up a hello to my father. No reply. I called again.

I & I

The scent of something slimy seeped out from under their bedroom door: fear. Fear perhaps of not being able to control something you have always been able to control, fear of losing what little is left of your manhood, or fear of being found hiding like a child. He must have heard the boots and thought tonight would be his pointy reckoning. Or that any conversation would lead to someone's death.

My mother crossed her arms. Her oval face zipped tight.

Should I go up and pull the coward out? Drag him down the stairs? Beat him? No. Violence is not the way to show my conviction to Maat (the ancient Egyptian religion based on truth, order and justice). Violence is "the simple, ultimate solution for economic competition," Tom Wolfe wrote in his essay "Pornoviolence." And as a senior partner at a white-shoe law firm explained about why he liked to hire women: "They work twice as hard for half as much."

This man upstairs, this man who never knew his father or his mother, who must have suffered far greater abuse than I, this man addicted to porn, this man who drove his family to Bear Mountain for outings, this man who would take a bullet for his friends, this king of the double shifts for as long as I could remember, this man who taught me to erase *can't* from my mental dictionary, and who once quoted Shakespeare to me: Until thine own self be true, how can anyone else be false? This same man was hiding. You could smell the fear.

Time to clarify the future. Clear new space. Dream of my own family. A new reality. One based not on fear and violence but on love and intelligence. In Betty Smith's classic novel, *A Tree Grows in Brooklyn*, the matriarch/soul of the book asks her good, first-born daughter why she has prohibited her other daughter, a promiscuous girl, from visiting her and her two young children. The eldest daughter sternly replies: "I have my own ways." The mother bows her head, lifts it and replies: "Forgiveness is the greatest gift we can give, and yet it is so inexpensive."

As I opened the door my mother spat out——-"I don't know why you're so upset!"

"Why are you screaming?" I asked calmly. She didn't say anything. I looked up the stairs and considered my father's behavior: At what age did his trauma stunt his maturity? Probably very early. I could not be mad at my parents. I loved them even more, because I knew in my heart that what had made them who they are had done far worse things to my ancestors. They had only treated me like America treated them. My parents had survived this neo-middle passage and done the best they could, instilling in me their values. Now it was up to me to sort the good from the bad, the conscious from the unconscious.

Looking back, "it was all good," as the Brooklyn rap Star Biggie Smalls would say about his poverty and jail experiences. Like, Biggie, I would learn from my negative experiences and hold no grudges, because there are kids who are going through experiences that are far worse, and although many times I had wished my parents would have gotten divorced, who knows how that would have worked out, for everyone. I had felt their divorce would have brought me to manhood much sooner, forcing me to accept more responsibility, which was something I lusted for. To be my own man. At night I would lay in my bed and play back the day's abuse trying to figure out why. I did not believe in God, but I would recite *Invictus*: "Black as the night that covers me, black as the pit in the deepest hole. No matter how straight the gate, how charged with punishment the scroll, I am the master of my fate, I am the captain of my soul." I had decided to be a yes man, I had decided to be silent, I had decided to beg, so the girls would not have to see me being beat anymore. It was not that I couldn't take the beating. Anyone can take a beat-down.

The humiliation was something else all together. Too see their pitying eyes in school the next day. . . . But just as I had made those choices and decided to lay against the ropes as I did my bid, when I wanted to, I did unleash the fury of my intelligence, the anger of my voice, and the truth of my spirit. The choice was always with me and the oppressors who guided their actions could not beat that freedom of will out of me. As I swung that 2X4, this was the lesson I had wanted him to learn: the spirit was dormant, not dead, it can strike like a cobra at anytime and kill.

"I think," I said to my mother standing in the doorway, "we should just admit that we have two different ways of living and move to the next level. This way, no one has any false expectations."

She seemed slightly stunned that I'd said that, and didn't reply. In high school I had met two guys who were going through similar experiences, one of the experiences involved incest and other barbarous acts. They convinced me not to run away from home. They convinced me that we could help each other get through it and reach for higher goals because: "The running away shit is a dead end," my boy Jay had said. "I know some guys who did it. They're on the pipe now, homeless, in gangs, in jail." For days, I thought about what they said and decided to stay and finish the four years remaining in my sentence. As my brothers and sisters finished high school, they found no reasons to come back home and many excuses as to why they could not. I had lived in a home with seven and sometimes eight people, but most of us had secret lives. It was as if we were living out President Clinton's "Don't ask, don't tell policy." I didn't want to start a family of my own that lived by such a rule. I did not want my own family to be ruled by fear. I wanted my family to be fueled and guided by love. And I knew it was possible from the black families that I knew. These were not the black families on the six o'clock news. The nightly news wanted nothing to do with wholesome black families. When I discovered these families, it was like a whole new world had opened up to me, and I felt greatly relieved and validated, because I knew they had existed, although growing up I had not seen them.

"Thanks for the photos," I said to my mother as I turned away, feeling the rush of Arctic air on my face. "Take care."

I tired to think about something else, not the strangeness coming over me, not the sense of weird separation. My cell rang.

"Hi...It went OK. No drama. I'll tell you when I get home. ...Yeah that sounds good."

I'd go home and watch the fight with the girl who would become my wife. We both felt Mike Tyson would demolish that kid from London. In the morning, I'd go to the gym and box, put in an extra hour. Put in some good work. Take out my frustrations. In a few years somebody would take the title from "Iron Mike," but not tonight.

I dipped my chin into my parka and marched toward the train station. The wind made it seem like February would last forever.

PROSE

6...Angel Dust: Fred Hampton

December 4, 1969
In the wee small hours
The sound of pigs

In the wee small hours
Loud snorts
A white Vietnam Vet wakes from his sleep screaming, tears
burning his lips, crying out: "He was only 21-years-old!"

Somewhere on the rez
a rattler's tail shakes fiercely

"Terminate"
With "Extreme Prejudice," as the cops say
No "It's the police! Open up!" cop-show bullshit
Just cold veins
And scorching bullets jacking into sleeping bodies
regardless of gender or state of pregnancy

12/4/69
a young Black man
with ideas about human rights, free breakfasts for kids and
education for all

living in the land of freedom and bravery
is a threat to society

John Coltrane's horn blares a long snarling note
Shells hit the wood floor of Fred's safe house
His body lifts with each bullet
Hundreds of bullets tear through plaster and wood and
flesh
A murderous symphony continues for over an hour
The Coltrane note gets louder, reaching a crescendo
As Fred and his girlfriend exhale their final
breath

12.4.69
London, Prague, Paris
all burning
Because of what Fred said
   Young kids rebel in the streets from Bed-Stuy to Brix-
ton, from Brownsville to Bahia
Because of what Fred Hampton said
   Cowards *sans* pointy white hoods came to his home
Because he looked innocent and good natured
   Assassins with shiny tin badges came
Because he could organize like Marx
   Centurians of European colonialism came
Because he had balls like Malcolm
   Little dick racists came all over themselves that night
Because he could orate like King
           and meet the same fate

I & I

December Fourth, Nineteen-sixty-nine
Twilight of the god
Fred Hampton is the reason my friends and I walk
unafraid of becoming strange fruit swinging from Southern trees
with our sex cut off

The neocolonialists said, "The white picket fence must be
maintained
At the cost of nothing:
The cost of Black life"

Black genius
An oxymoronic phrase
Like America liberty

"We don't give a damn how many thousands of mouths
Fred feeds with that
breakfast program of his.
We don't care if his worst crime *was* playing Robin Hood
with an ice cream
truck on a hot July day.
We don't give a shit if his politics are evolving, shithead!
That red and black bastard is going to get it like the St.
Valentine's day massacre!
We are Hoover, Daley, Corcoran, Bull Connor, and COIN-
TELPRO et al—
So get the fuck out of the way—
We're going to dispense justice
We're going to give that coon a wake up call
at 4:30 a.m. on the morning of December 4th

In the year of our Lord nineteen hundred and sixty-nine
A wake up call he'll never remember!"

Xenophobia
Ethnocentrism

"Freedom ain't free!
And despite what Mr. Hampton fed you, those breakfasts
were very expensive
And we pigs are so bad
So mutherfucking badass
We will drug a black fool with our lies and teach him self-
hatred and how to shoot
And have a good ol' laugh while he mows his brother
down
We will blast in there with our big black guns and our
Big black fool
And we will find that Fred motherfucking Hampton
And God help whoever else is in there
Because it's Zulu time
And we are in country."

"You can kill a revolutionary!" Fred once told a packed
auditorium of supporters and fellow Panthers. "But you
cannot kill a revolution!"

Later that morning
An old woman
Wearing all black

I & I

Walked along Chicago's icy ghetto streets
The wind was raw and unforgiving
The air was dusted white from a light snow
Ghosts of the dead flew in the streets
The woman wore a black veil to mask hot tears
She stood outside the house riddled by over a thousand bullets

Weeping
She clutched at the cold slippery railing
She looked at the ram-shackled house blanketed by gloom
tears started anew and she lost her grip
She fell to one knee
And crumbled in the snow
The choking Lake Michigan winds cut off her air and stung her face
She felt her hip turn the color purple
She cried out bitterly, "Lord! He was only 21-years-old!"
and pounded her fist on the powdery concrete

Hoover, Daley, Connor, Corcoran
COINTELPRO et al
dispensed justice
On the morning of December 4ᵗʰ, 1969
Judge jury executioner
Killed the morning glory
Killed the serpentine fire

The old woman felt a strong arm lifting her up,
she felt the young stranger's gentle embrace
as he helped her to her feet

She lifted her veil to thank him
But he was gone

NOTE: For Fred's son, the struggle continues...

For Sandra

PROSE

7...Wild Thing

The original wild thing was the pharaoh of the Armana period. This heretic king was not down for the idealized paintings and sculptures that you see in many museums. He kept it real. He was also not down for the corrupt priests, who had made themselves and their minor Gods more powerful than the pharaoh and *thee* God, Ra, Or Amun-Ra if you will. This pharaoh dragged Egypt kicking and screaming back to monotheism and weakened the priesthood. So the priests conspired to assassinate him and did, viciously—"You fuckin' cripple! Now you're really a cripple!" After bashing in his head with rocks, they also killed his loving wife, the exquisitely beautiful and graceful Nefertiti (which means "the beautiful one coming toward you"). These priests/haters never liked the fact that the dazzling Nefertiti was with such an ugly, weak-looking and pot-bellied pharaoh, who also had a mildly crooked spine, who spent his free time writing hymns to his children, playing with his children in the palace garden and writing poetry in praise of Ra. What most people don't know is that this pharaoh had a son, who was wilder than hell and who, by age 18, had mastered all the manly and mystical arts. The son of the heretic king was all about expanding Egypt's borders. At 13, this boy could make his alternate body, his ba, travel to different parts of the world. Astral travel was a rare feat for someone so new to the Egyptian Mystery System, but let's just say he had a gift. When this son became pharaoh at age 16, he did not have to ask what happened to his father, he had already witnessed it first hand. And upon returning from the past to his physical form in the present, he wept uncontrollably. He did not have to ask what had happened to his mother, he had already seen it. And he could not be consoled. He went to his tutor and asked, "What shall I do?" The scribe/priest told him, "Your fate has already been determined by your character," and turned his back on the boy. The priest, who had tutored the boy's father, had known the young pharaoh all his life. This priest walked away, clear streams cascading silently over high dark cheek bones. This boy king could race a chariot and fight like no one had ever seen. This handsome boy invited all 12 of his parents' assassins out on a lion hunting party one day and hunted them down with his huge bows and arrows. Then he did to them what you do to dead prey that you wish to eat. But they were not dead. Two years later he came home from a mining expedition exhausted, went to sleep and had a dream. When he awoke he went to see his girlfriend, his Heaven on Earth. They laughed and talked and made love, and he asked his one true love to thrown him a party. "Because tomorrow I will die," he said smiling. His princess laughed and caressed his smooth yet already care-worn face, the face already showing the signs of the burden of empire. She tried to smooth away the worries that were already apparent on his young but furrowed brow. She told him not to make such morbid jokes. She thought him far too young to die and far too strong mentally, physically and spiritually to be killed. In truth, she thought him invincible. He was her God. In fact, she had seen him kill far bigger men with his bare hands. It was she who had taught him the concepts of compassion and mercy, because all grace in those matters seemed foreign to him. He was born a wild animal it seemed at many times. Yet, she threw him a lavish party anyway, thinking he was making another one of his morbid jokes. He seemed to have a preoccupation with death, but since he had met her, he had begun to have a preoccupation with life. As he slept the next night, he heard his guards slipping away from their posts, as they were paid exorbitantly to do. He heard his assassins coming to execute their plot: to bash in his skull, like their fellow priests had bashed in his father's. He felt the poison taking violent effect in his system, and as if in a dream, his spirit lifted away from him, into his princess's womb, giving their child life.

Wild Thing

When I was a teen, my hair, unlike me, was wild and uncontrollable. I loved my hair but it didn't love me. No matter how often I combed it, it soon turned into a lumpy landscape comprising three different textures. It also grew with a startling quickness and thickness that annoyed me. As you can imagine, my Afro in the '70s was not the envy of my friends (who envied the strong and silent, kick-ass character, Link, on *The Mod Squad*). Nor was my wig the one that made the girls in Junior High School coo (that was reserved for pre-plastic surgery Michael Jackson, the b-ballers on *The White Shadow* and neon-smile Duane on *What's Happening*). Before I hit my teens, my barber would often tell me matter-of-factly, "Ya know, you're going bald," as he pointed to a shadow of an elongated diamond in the center of my crown. I could see it, but I never wanted to believe it. As usual, I thanked him for his fascinating observation.

Then one day when I was 15, the front of my hairline started receding, and the next thing you know—I hit college looking like George Jefferson. I had a hair transplant, which looks—let me tell ya—*wonderful*, very "Hey, baby doll," with the dotted hairline to match (call that decision the wisdom of youth). Now, I have a little on top at the front, but none on the crown. I didn't complete the transplant because the surgery/drilling was just too much fun. So I keep it low and groomed. Now—the strangest thing in the world, and quite naturally—it's growing back, wild and uncontrollable.

For Nefertiti

PROSE

8...Got Milk?

On our last visit to the public pool, I nibbled on an orange while watching my parents splash and frolic. The sun shimmered off their bronze shoulders. They laughed like the 19-year-olds they were when they first met. My father had flirted like a man in love at first sight, chatting up my mother for three hours nonstop, hoping all the while he would not put his foot in his mouth. When my mother rolled up her immaculate white towel (the cleanliness of which impressed my father) and placed it in her straw bag, my father asked if he could see her again. She was reluctant because she knew of him, and knew he had a lot of girlfriends; she didn't want or need another playa. She smiled briefly: "Oh, you'll see me again. I'm here all the time." My father went back to the pool every day after work for two weeks, but never again saw his mermaid. On his last futile visit, his shoulders sagged as he stepped out of the pool house with his head down, bumping straight into her.

Now, as parents, they worked around the clock, so it was great to see them finally having some fun. It was the last time.

At the Kingston airport, I wore white linen and distress. My mother brushed away an almost unnoticeable and salty watermark; straightened the lapel of the white suit she had sewn for me; caressed my back: "Everything will be OK, Honey." As the plane ascended on its diagonal trajectory, my ears began to ache and pop. I breathed through my mouth and chewed gum, as I had been instructed by my mother, both helped. Looking out the oval window, the gently swaying palm trees faded . . . to light, purplish blue skies. I fell softly to sleep. My imagination re-played bloody fears. I awoke screaming, my head banging against the window. The middle-aged man behind me wailed like a mourner who had lost his wife, which made sense, since his wife was having a heart attack. As she convulsed, tiny white particles swirled against the black sky, like the falling confetti at the annual Halloween-type parade in Kingston, Jamaica's capitol city. I had always watched the parade, called Jonkunu (*jon-KUN-new*), with awe and fear. The horrific masks of the dancers and their frightening chalky-white and multicolored body paint, augmented by the ominous frenetic music, made me feel like I was watching a scary obeia ritual, something I had overheard older kids gossiping about. One of the brightly plumed dancers would invariably spot me cowering behind a post office box, and jump into my face—-"Boo!"—-sending me bawling home on my scooter. But now I felt really scared. The falling stewards frantically tried to attend to the man's dying wife. Her chest heaved up and down. Her eyes rolled out of sight. Then she lost consciousness.

The plane tossed like a salad. It felt like a rapidly descending and ascending roller-coaster or a free-falling elevator. I knew we were all in death's clutch. My testicles were shooting up to my throat. I didn't know where my mother or brothers and sisters were in all the chaos of people moving and falling about. I was afraid my mother and family were going to die, and I looked for her crying because I wanted to save her. I turned around. I was sure the woman behind me was going to be dead in a few seconds. I didn't care about myself. I couldn't see my mother, but I knew she was probably trying to make sure we were all safe. As

I crawled around, my internal organs shot up through my body and seemed to be separating from their bolts. With each jolt of the plane, everything in my body took hard thrusts upward. My internal organs felt like they were going to shoot through my head. Carry-on luggage shot out of holding areas and flew. The captain continually tried to reassure us that the "turbulence" would soon end.

"Laud God!" many replied, "save me! Mossey me God!" The strength of safety belts strained to the breaking point with each sudden jerk or drop, and snapped free. "We gun crash! We gun die!" The screams intensified to deafening as the plane spiraled down, crashing onto the snow covered tarmac of the newly named John F. Kennedy International Airport. We skidded off the snow-packed runway, colliding into the side of a hanger. Passengers jolted forward, crunching bloodily into seat backs. Some people, like me, flew. I couldn't move or feel my legs, and I screamed my head off at thought of being cripple.

All of us were dazed, fractured, bruised, shell-shocked, or worse. I was now numb, quiet and twisted up, because this was what I had expected, except that I had dreamt the plane would go down in a fiery heap, unlike a phoenix. As the attendants and emergency ground crews got things sorted, an EMS technician with a reassuring smile dislodged me from between two collapsed seats ("Ah, you're alright," she said. "You're young. You're a tough guy!"). She lifted me too my feet, which were working, but wobbly. I thought feeling my legs was nothing short of miracle. "Hardly a bruise on ya," the Emergency Service Technicians (EMS) said smiling, patting me on the back. They wheeled around a shaky metal staircase, and everyone who could, deplaned on their own. Some people were brought out laced to stretchers, but none that I could see had white sheets covering their faces. My family and I slipped and staggered down the stairs, which instilled as much confidence as the flight. We were like pin-balls buffeted against the staircase's icy aluminum railings by the ice storm; the fierce wind cut off our oxygen. Ice shards stung our faces like bees. Driving snow choked the black sky. All around us was nothing but black night. The snow blew in every direction. Hot tears streamed down the faces of my brothers and sisters. We were entering America 2 days before Christmas, in the Age of Aquarius, the Age of Love: 1969, harmony, understanding, assassinations. In 1969, America was in love with the rose and the revolver. In the Age of Aquarius, after the assassination of President John F. Kennedy, baseball's Mets had made Americans believe in amazing miracles again. And new President Lyndon Johnson's Great Society program, my parents' reason for immigrating, would soon fade like palm trees to azure skies, as purple as a fading bruise. The peace-loving flower children who danced and smoked "pot" and had casual sex were the opposite of the demonic Manson clan, which had massacred a Hollywood director and his guests in their sleep two weeks earlier.

As my seven-member family struggled toward the customs terminal, fighting for every inch against the hurricane wind, which suddenly died, turning from violent to gentle. Soft violins played from somewhere in the coal night. I stuck out my tongue and enjoyed my first snowflake. The melting sensation filled me with joy. I stopped crying and smiled. I felt so good, so alive, that I jumped in the air. It was like hearing music or having fun for the first time. The tension in my body slipped away, like a departing boat's cast-off rope. The snowflakes melted in my mouth lighter than air. In its taste, I don't know why, I felt God, and believed in God for the first time. This momentary sensation erased everything bad that had happened. I started skating on the icy snow.

"Come on!" my frazzled mother yelled, yanking me forward, trying to keep all her trembling and frightened ducks in a row.

"Why did we come here?" I demanded in my 9-year-old voice, now jolted back to reality, and trying to make sense of leaving what I considered paradise.

"For better opportunities!" she snapped loudly, more concerned about getting us through customs without being strip-searched by power-tripping Fischer-Pryce cops. It seemed the customs agents thought all Jamaicans smoked "pot," and like the American Express card, we wouldn't leave home without it.

The next day, I began fourth grade in Bed-Stuy, Brooklyn. Before the first bell, angelic faces on the playground chanted with homicidal anger—"Ungowa! Black Power! Des-troy, white boy! I said it! I meant it! And I'm here to rep-re-sent it!' I was taught by my *new best friends* that Black Panther leaders Huey Newton and Bobby Seale were courageous, charismatic and cool. The Panthers' elementary-school breakfast programs, and their armed defiance of police brutality, were much admired. My schoolmates looked up to the young black men and women who would die for them, who gave them a voice on the national stage, that is, the nightly TV news. On a grassroots level, these were the same type of young women and men who fed them breakfast, ensuring that they would have a hot meal before starting school. The Panthers brazenly challenged America's overt and covert war on African-Americans, opened free health clinics, and read the great philosophers. Many of them, like 21-year-old Fred Hampton, were magnificent, incredibly stirring orators. Many of them, like Fred, were assassinated. The Panthers filled America's air with heady ideas and the belief that the world could change. Incarcerated Panther leader Eldridge

Cleaver wrote *Soul on Ice* from prison and mandated that America must change or die, for when you hold down one thing, you hold down the adjoining. Fanning the flames of my classmates' hatred were unrelenting news reports of assassinations: the four little girls, their peers, killed in the Birmingham church bombing; in the previous summer, the Nobel Peace prize-winner, the reverend Dr. Martin Luther King Jr., had been assassinated by a white male. Several months after his murder, Senator Bobby Kennedy, a symbol of white American goodness and hope for equality, was assassinated by a white male—as his hope-inspiring brother, America's prince charming, President John F. Kennedy (of the recently re-named airport), had been five years earlier. America's holy trinity—Kennedy, King, Kennedy—-had been crucified by little dick Klansmen, or so my classmates thought, and my classmates believed that there would be no Resurrection of the holy trinity. No renewal, no spring, only an unending "hazy shade of winter": unrelenting seasons of gun smoke and tear gas. It didn't matter to them that two of the three photos on their grandmothers' living-room walls were white.

In my classmates' rooms were three different photos. First and always, the lean, suited, black liberation leader Malcom X, cautiously peering out from behind a window curtain looking for assassins, while holding an equally sleek automatic assault rifle. (The caption below the photo read "Self-Defense By Any Means Necessary.") The second photo was of a 21-year-old Muhammad Ali standing over the brutish, late-30-something Sonny Liston, whom Ali had just knocked down, and was screaming to get up! In the photo, Ali's a well-muscled arm is curled, urging Liston to get up: the veins in his huge curled bicep bulged phenomenally. Liston, the mafia's boy, was thought unbeatable until Ali destroyed him. Ali became the heavyweight champion of the world that night and exclaimed loudly and repeatedly while jumping on the ropes and pointing out to the audience: "I shook up the world!" Ali was soon stripped of his championship title for refusing to be drafted for the Vietnam War. Ali, a member of Malcolm X's Nation of Islam, objected on religious grounds and stated that he wasn't going half-way around the world to kill people he had no quarrel with, especially when black people right here in America were "catching hell." In the Age of Aquarius, the Age of Love, what singer Billie Holiday called "strange fruit" could still be found swinging from Southern trees, their genitals cut out by klansmen, so could black men tied to trees with heavy chains that tore gullies into their flesh, men who had been beaten to a pulp and had their genitals removed. This is what fueled my classmates' hate.

The third and last photo in my classmates' rooms would always be of the handsome Panther leader Huey Neuton, seated in a high, round-back wicker chair, holding an armed rifle in one hand and a spear in the other. Neuton also wore a black leather jacket, a black beret roguishly tilted down to the left, with mean-looking ammo belts slung across his chest in an X pattern. He too shook up the world. The bad-ass black men on the national stage were just getting started. They had hit threshold with the racist bullshit. They were going to end the 600 years of oppression by any means necessary. On that June day when the Panthers marched into governor Ronald Reagan's California state house strapped with armed shotguns and rifles to protest the repeal of the right to openly bear arms, white American gulped and held their breath. Brothers ready to set it were coming right into white America's living room, live and in living color.

With each passing day in 1969, anger grew in my classmates' bedrooms, while sorrow blossomed in their grandmothers' living-rooms.

What happens to a dream deferred the Harlem poet Langston Hughes asked? The coming-of-age Baby Boom generation (the large numbers of white and black babies born after World War II) raged in armed rebellion against homicidal racism, against elected leaders opposed to freedom for all, and against the Vietnam War draft, which sent their working-class buddies half way around the world to kill people of color they didn't even know, and for purposes, the Boomers suspected, that would only benefit America's wealthiest 1 percent. Rifles and revolvers were grabbed by Boomers of all colors. The Jews, who had occupied the same space as blacks in the minds of bigots, also had beef. Jews weren't allowed into the Ivy League in any real numbers until the 1960s. The Boomers marched in civil and un-civil disobedience to change the nation by peace or force, often quoting their icon of rebellion and self-determination, the towering intellectual Malcolm X, who also dominated the media's stage. On a news program, Malcolm and Harlem writer James Baldwin had made the U.S. Senate look intellectually inferior and ignorant when they had testified about race relations. The Boomers used the temerity and intelligence of their heroes and icons to give them courage to fight and tenacity to persevere. The Boomers stopped traffic, took over the streets and chanted with seemingly unlimited energy against the Vietnam War. "Power to Young People!" They burned their draft cards in front of the "pigs!"/cops. They spat on military personnel (many of whom had grown up adoring "Big John Wayne's" nationalistic movies, while simultaneously learning to believe in America's right without questioning its actions). They chanted with fist-pumping fury against the "pretty boy's" ugly successor Lyndon Baines Johnson: "Hey! Hey! L-B-J! How Many Kids Have You Killed Today?!" President Johnson, a former senator from the lone star state, had continued to send troops to Vietnam even as he knew, with each passing day, that it was a war America could not win. But his Texas-sized ego would not let him be the first American president to lose a war, and so boys from poor black and white neighborhoods continued to die. Blacks and Latinos were placed on the front lines in significantly disproportionate numbers and died in those numbers. This also fed my classmates' hate. It was America's longest war, and as the death toll for American soldiers and Vietnamese increased, the latter to over 4 million—American white youth wondered if it was not time to really get down. White youth answered their own questions by forming peaceful and unpeaceful organizations to end the Vietnam War. The mad bombers of the Weathermen Underground blew up government buildings in retaliation to the War and what they considered to be oppressive acts, such as the massacre of the innocent villagers at Mei Lei in Vietnam. Their days of rage would continue well into the 1970s. They felt, "We got to knock these motherfuckers who control this shit right on their ass!" They did not like seeing their friends and relatives coming home maimed and mutilated, or watching them be destroyed on the nightly news. It was the longest war in U.S. history, and for the young white men and women of the Weather Underground, it was going to end now by any means necessary. They marched on the Pentagon and brought the fight directly to the powers that be. These were the days when kids in China, Japan, France and Angola were doing the same exact thing. They all spoke with one voice, and it was loud and it was angry.

But president Johnson knew order at home had to be kept, so the anti-war protestor and heroic symbol, the boxer Muhammad Ali, was stripped of his heavyweight title for five-years during the prime of his boxing career. Firemen blasted high pressure hoses at the Boomers crashing them into walls, where ravenous police attack dogs were waiting for them. German Shepherds ravaged their flesh while they were down, and "the pigs" clubbed the Boomers with nightsticks as their fellow police officers shot the War protesters, some of whom were armed, some of whom were not. It was hard to tell in the hazy shade of winter: the swirl of tear gas. The shooting of students by police at Kent State College was the most publicized of such legalized massacres, next to assasination of Black Panther leader Fred Hampton and his associates in the still of December night, when homicide came in force and without out so much as a polite knock at the door. Massacres also happened at black colleges, but went unreported in mainstream media. There was more than enough violence on white campuses to keep Main Street media shocked and busy. Formerly peaceful students now started attending funerals for their friends, and responded to the police attacks by strapping on AK-47s, and double-barrel shotguns, and taking over administration buildings at Ivy League universities like Cornell and Columbia. The war at home was on.

On the grainy black-and-white news each night, urban cities and college campuses looked like firewood ablaze. Everyone on both sides of the war was down for whatever—whatever it takes to win and by any means necessary.

In my elementary school, I learned from my deskmate, Vance, that Bed-Stuy was called "the Do or Die." I volunteered to be milk monitor to get a better lay of the land and to get a break from the kids making fun of my "F-O-B" (Fresh Off the Boat) Jamaican accent. So before I punched somebody out on my first day, I bounced. I also wanted to get a break from the kiddie chorus gleefully singing about my sneakers ("Rejects, they cost a $1.99! Rejects—they make your feet feel fine! Rejects! Oh, get your Rejects! Oh, get your Rejects! Your Rejects! Todaaay-aaaay!"). Kids doubled over in laughter at the song's end. It didn't help that my new Rejects were already ripping at their canvas corners. I felt poor and worthless, but I knew I would find a way to win. I just had to find it soon. I felt like I was being given a crash course in whom to trust and hate—and I better not disagree. I better conform. It felt like I was caught between walls closing in on me—and I didn't like it. It was just like the terrifying claustrophobia you feel when you are on an airplane that you know is going to crash. Your fate is sealed.

In the hallway, the strong scent of first-day-of-school floor wax filled the air. Up ahead of me, I spied the old stooped janitor, tiredly pushing his mop and four-wheel bucket, exhausted from life's unwon battles. The weighty meat cleaver in his back pocket sagged his green work chinos down and to the left.

I pushed open the brown wooden "Boys' Bathroom" door and stepped around a puddle the color of a rose. The blood was thick, with an almost raw smell. I couldn't take my eyes off it as I washed my hands in the cracked sink. I was shocked and amazed. How had it been drained so neatly into such a perfect "O"? What had happened? Who did it? I got the sense that the janitor carried a meat cleaver for his own protection. Earlier, on my way to school, this kid had said, "Yo, lend me a quarter," as an introduction to a mugging. I kicked him in the balls and stepped, not thinking twice about it, except for the fleeting thought that he must have been crazy to think I was going to give him my money. More culture shock followed as I had entered the schoolyard and saw the angelic amber faces chanting loud and proud. I was a long way from my little school room in Kingston, where you only feared getting hit with the teacher's ruler for messing up your lessons.

As I walked through the halls now, the visions of heinous murder and torture I had while sleeping on the plane re-played in mind. I scanned the glass cases, wondering if, thinking about death would bring it, or if it was a premonition I could escape. I hadn't know anyone who had died or been killed. I had only seen death in the American movies I had snuck into back in J-A., and in the rough Jamaican movie about a young singer trying to make it in the reggae-music scene called *The Harder They Come.* Yeah, he fell hard.

The glass cases in the hallway were filled with "Year 2000" prize drawings of futuristic buildings, which looked mostly like stuff from the space-age *Jetsons* cartoon; next to those were gold-starred essays on the meaning of Christmas; and water-color illustrations of rosy-cheeked Dick and Jane skipping off to school, with their smiling, tongue-wagging beagle, "Spot," running after them.

The intoxicating smell of mimeograph ink met me as I rounded the corner, along with a row of miniature flags—British Columbia, Poland, Japan—yet no black, yellow and green? I wondered how I could fit in. Did I have any long-lost family in the South? I walked on, reading glass-enclosed announcements on official rules of conduct, times and rooms for reading labs, and the seemingly endless honor roll, which I paused at, scanning the names, doubting that I would ever make the cut. As I continued walking, my mind returned to the boys' bathroom and the perfect red circle on the white square tiles. . . . .

"BETTY," that's what her nametag read. She was a 40-something kitchen worker who looked twice her age. Her face was full of flaps and folds, drawn down by years of sadness. She pushed me the box of graham crackers and half-pints without noticing me, contemplating far more serious things. My sneakers seemed insignificant. Then she sighed, with a heavy heart, as she began to once again stir a vat of hot chicken soup, its aromatic steam rising.

Walking out of the empty lunchroom, a fellow student grabbed me in a headlock from behind. He was a few inches taller than me, maybe a 6th grader. I couldn't see him, but he smelled like dirt and the funk of sweat.

"Up the milk!" His forearm tightened under my chin in an iron grip and yanked it up.

Sharp steel pressed into my throat. I felt the blood and froze from the shock, and a terror that possessed me to my quivering core. The seven-inch "007" slid across deeper, painlessly at first. Standing there in stunned disbelief, I clutched my burning throat as he raced away with the milk and crackers; I could hear the rubber of his sneakers squeak sharply as he sprinted away on the newly waxed floors. Hot blood gushed between my fingers, hitting the gleaming floor. Twin thoughts echoed in my mind: kill him; and then, he must have been really hungry. I felt sorry for him. Things slowed. I felt myself rising out of myself, my body fading, my knees jelly, my eyelids so heavy, seeing only the color of coal and swirling white ash. . . .

My friend Vance watched me playing football in the schoolyard during recess the following semester.

"Damn!" Vance said, giving me a pound after my leaping touchdown catch, "you came back with a vengeance!"

I took a knee, crossed myself and said a prayer, something I would do throughout my collegiate career. I got up thanking God, thought about my recent academic success, and felt my smooth neck. The young plastic surgeons had wanted to make a name for themselves. They made the deep wide gash invisible. They described my quick and complete recovery as "nothing short of remarkable!" I had learned in the hospital that He had made me an example. Now He expected more. Now He expected leadership. Lying on the hospital bed with a tangle of tubes sprouting out of my nose, mouth, neck and wrist, watching the neon green LED sprout little green pyramids on the black screen, He told me that He wanted me to *try* to do everything better and to not be afraid of my surroundings and what was happening to me, although it might look like certain death.

"Let no one put fear in your heart!" He commanded menacingly. He was angry at me: "Think not of what you can hate about people, but what you can love about them." He wanted me to reshape my broken sinful mass into a life of love: He said, lovingly then, "Grow beyond your broken and sinful self my son, have compassion for the pain of others, have tolerance for what is beyond you. Live, as I love."

I tell this story to you because He asked me to.

The last thing I remember from that night in the hospital was a soft hand brushing over my forehead and closing my eyes. "I see all and hear all."

As He did this I saw, in the center of a street, a white pyramid with blotches of black, almost like cow spots. I would see this pyramid again while in Italy on my honeymoon, near the Circus Maximus, the home of the gladiators. A chill passed over me.

For Monika

PROSE

9...Shining Serpent

The Fictional Life and Death of Tupac Amaru Shakur
(June 16, 1971—September 13, 1996)

A noon tide have you been our twilight, and your youth has given us dreams to dream/No stranger are you among us, nor a guest, but our son and dearly beloved/Suffer not yet our eyes to hunger for your face. . . .

Earlier that night in the presidential suite, Suge (pronounced *Shug, as in Sugar Bear*) had glared murderously at Pac, shouting—"What!?"

Suge Knight, the president of Pac's record company, is a massive, NFL-sized guy, whose coal eyes resemble those of a hired killer.

Pac, at 5'10 was wiry but well muscled. He sat across the room like a volcano, puffing on a cigarette, like he was about to get up and kick Suge's big ass, but he was trying to be cool—but fuck it, he wasn't giving Suge control of his masters. Not under any circumstances!

"You heard me muthaucka!" Pac shouted without looking at Suge. "I didn't stutter!"

"Shut up, nigga! You gon get down or you gon lay down!"

The ex-gang member and owner of Death Row Records meant that Pac could get down with the program or lay down for his final rest.

Pac ripped up an antique writing table and threw it across the room. He stalked over to the fireplace, where the Sugar Bear stood ready to do damage. Pac got up in his face, which was fearsome enough to scare Charles Manson. Pac's ripped shoulders lifted up and rounded forward like an lion about to attack its prey. His eyes were on fire. Suge drew his Desert Eagle from its holster and pushed it into Pac's shirtless chest, pushing him backward.

Pac shrugged nonchalantly and pointed his own Desert Eagle to Suge's dome.

"Now what, be-otch," Pac said calmly . . . I ain't Dre, nigga!" Pac was referring to the strong-arm tactics Suge had used to obtain Dr. Dre's early masters. As Pac's pistol aimed at Suge's forehead, the 15 people in the entourage held their breaths. The tension had gotten thick quick. Double homicide time. I pulled out my own Calico, because he wasn't shooting my boy. Fuck that. Let the chips fall in Vegas motherfuckas.

Pac said, "This nigger ain't missed since the third grade, so what you wanna do?"

Suge's extensive belly lifted up and down as he laughed a deep bass laugh, like this nigger's so crazy and it was all a big joke. He lowered his gun and backed up. He was a businessman first and foremost, and Pac, a hip-hop and movie star, was his ticket to staying in the double "R" (Rolls Royce) life.

Pac shoved his Desert Eagle down into the front of his baggie jeans before turning to one of Suge's flunkies and yelling, "Clean this fucking place up! Now, motherfucka!" Pac began kicking stuff all over the place, including the flunky, whose body lifted up off the floor with each kick to his midsection. Suge just laughed. The issue of who owned the masters was settled, for now.

I & I

I put the Calico, *with the black talons loaded in the clip*, back in my shoulder holster. When I was packing to come out here the steel was the last thing I packed. I had been reading all about my boy from childhood days and had a bad feeling that I would need it. I hadn't carried it anywhere in a long time, except to target practice. In Harlem, we say if you carry it, you will use it. As I put holes in paper heads I had wondered about the latest US public enemy. Was Pac the psycho brother many assumed he was? Or was he hip hop's Bob Marley? Or was there more to the story of the kid I had rolled with in elementary and hung with in our building on 122nd and Morningisde in Manhattan?

Some would call him a trickster: an African literary icon who confounds as he informs. Pac's body of soul music received carefully selected play on air waves, so only a certain image of Pac was allowed to emerge. This image was, at best, as a thug with a heart of gold. This was a familiar trope in the imagination of American pop culture, but I suspected that there was much more than the media's neat representation of a young black male in a straightjacket. I had lost touch with Pac after high school except for intermittent emails, so I wasn't sure if he was the same Pac I had known growing up.

"Anyone who has made contact with the world's myth's and spiritual's traditions will be more than familiar with the universal character of the Trickster," wrote Dustin Eaton in *Paraboloa*. "He is the one for whom the laws of causality are mere suggestions—a figure who brings forth monumental changes in both individual psyche and society at large. The Trickster is a clown and a madman, a shapeshifter and a psychopomp.... The techniques at his disposal are as varied as they are effective. Anything that will shock us out of our everyday perceptions and force us to view our lives from a different perspective can be a tool used by the Trickster. In the hands of a maestro like the

Trickster this powder keg we call existence is actually fun. He is able to ride the waves of instability while the rest of us sink to the bottom, pulled under by an anchor of depression. Hindus like to say that the Goddess is playful, and that life is her game. The Trickster would agree whole-heartedly. Unfortunately, the Trickster's gifts are not always packaged so pleasantly. Sometimes it takes tragedy to sound the alarm that we are taking our lives too seriously and too much for granted. Losing one's retirement fund to the roll of a roulette wheel [read as the wheel of fate] is one good example of the Trickster's most painful lesson—that life is indeed full of suffering. His final message is that order and chaos are not contradictory powers that one must constantly struggle with, but complimentary aspects of the same reality. In the end, confusion and clarity, comedy and tragedy, truth and illusion are just two sides of the same coin, constantly spinning." Like the wheel of fate. A "pscyhopomp is a patron of orphans and lost souls, a conductor of souls to the place of the dead." In Egyptian lore, he is the royal child, Anpu, the jackal-headed god who guides deceased souls through the underworld to the double hall of judgement and the scales of Maat. Metaphorically, the Anpu (known as Anubis to the Greeks) guided the sun safely through its underworld passage each night. Defender of the Truth, Guardian of the Secrets and the Sacred Writings, he is the Messenger.

I wasn't sure if Pac had become the nation's latest Trickster, but I would soon find out.

Now, driving in Vegas' balmy desert night, with Suge at the wheel of the *Bad Mon Wagon (BMW)*, Pac riding shotgun and me in the back, the attitude was more relaxed. Suge had given Pac's bodyguard and friend the night off. Pac's protégés, the 7-member rap group the Outlawz, most of whom were distant relations to Pac, trailed behind us in a gleaming black Cadillac Escalade truck. We'd all just come from watching Pac's running buddy, former heavyweight champion Mike Tyson, knock out some no-name in the first round. Mike had stalked over to his opponent like a robot and demolished him in a fury of thunderous blows that were painful to watch.

At the red light, a mild breeze blew through the blue BMW's windows, mixing with the blasting AC. The combination of fake and real air felt luxurious and strangely soothing.

"These seats," Pac exclaimed, rubbing the supple creamy leather, "are nicer than what most people got in their homes." Suge smiled approvingly. For a moment you might of thought Suge was a nice guy. As the corner of his smile faded you could see the trace of his menacing alter-ego, unable to be completely masked. The inky sky and soothing air made it feel like we were in the Tropics. Stars twinkled through the 745's sun-roof. We were all feeling good. Pac had let go of his earlier belligerent mood; the pugilist was at rest. Suge joked about all the girls Pac had rocked, and how many more he would as a result of Pac's forthcoming album, *Makavelli*, which was, by all early reviews, excellent.

I said, "All Pac ever needed to get a honey was five minutes." Pac smiled that Colgate smile of his that had always made my girlfriends wonder what it would be like to sleep with him. Then Pac sang the beautiful rapper Amil's famous line: "Yeah, 'but how we gonna get around on your bus pass.'" We all laughed, remembering that Pac was several times homeless early in his life and career; and the last time he had to wear bikini briefs and simulate fucking a blow-up doll on stage just to get money to eat. After months on the streets, that first real meal, as basic as it was, tasted like a delicious Thanksgiving feast.

Pac had felt the harsh dramatic irony of living in L.A., the quintessential the land of luxury, but living on the street and trying to ration his change for meals of bagels and oranges (Like the song says, "To live and die in L.A."—but for real though).

Now it was a different story. Suge and Pac were both young, gifted and very much in the black. The ganja, rolled in soft to-bacco leaf, tasted gentler and sweeter than the night air.

Pac tilted his head to the side, unable to hold back a small smile. He glanced at himself in the side mirror, allowing himself a small vanity. "We'll see how the CD does," he said matter of factly. But he didn't like the reflection. Having known Pac for so long, I could tell the wheels were spinning crazy fast in his head, although he appeared to be thinking about very little. He was probably considering who to hire as his new accounting firm, who to employ as his new lawyer, how the hell to he get off of this lawsuit-plagued label, Death Row Records, all things which we had talked about when he met me at the "Welcome to Las Vegas" sign and immediately sparked a blunt. "My nigga Ses! What up, baby boy!" I told him how two brothers we had known since grade school had died in police custody, but it didn't make the papers because they had been homeless. "I guess," Pac said facetiously, "it wasn't 'fit to print.' But I make the infotainment news nightly. Ain't that a bitch!"

Now, Suge shouted, "Triple platinum, nigga—that's what we gon see!"

Although I silently agreed with Suge's sales forecast, we laughed off Suge's false bravado. "This nigga," we said in uni-son.

Pac was confident about everything. The tracks on the new album were Pac's loudest, rawest and hardest, dramatizing the cutthroat existence and threadbare lives of America's silent ma-jority, blacks and whites who have not. Pac had asked me to come to Vegas to hang, because he needed someone he could "trust, someone who didn't want equity." I told him I had no way to get out there, since I fear flying and was strapped for cash in my recurring role as a starving artist. Pac sent me an Amtrak ticket and a Benz. Secretly, I feared hanging with him. Since he had become famous, violence followed him like night followed day. But where we come from, you're either all the way down or you're not.

Now, as we waited for the light to change at Flamingo and Coval, a less populous area of downtown, Suge blasted the old school joint from Grandmaster Flash and the Furious Five: "Don't push me too far, I'm close to the edge! I'm try-ing not to lose my head! It's like a jungle sometimes. It makes me wonder how I keep from going under! It's like a jungle sometimes. . . ."

A white sport Cadillac pulled up a little ahead of us as the light turned yellow. Poking out of its back window was a thin black metal pipe followed by thirteen shots sprayed directly at Pac. He struggled to pull his .4-5, but four shots found his right hand, pelvis and chest. The Cadillac screeched away, tires smok-ing, before the light turned green. The rap group the Outlawz, who looked up to Pac as a father figure, chased it, their guns blasting from all windows. They blew out the Caddy's back win-dow, but lost the car in a chase in congested downtown. The Outlawz had emptied their backup clips. No bullets hit Suge or me.

"Tupac Amaru"—Incan for "Shining Serpent"—fought for his life for seven days before dying on Friday the 13th. Tupac's mother Alfeni had named him after an Incan warrior chief.

In a prophetic eulogy from the supernova's posthumously released album *Makavelli, The Don Killuminati*, Pac wrote, "Don't shed a tear for me nigga, I ain't happy here/I hope they bury me and send me to my rest/Headlines reading Murdered to Death, my last breath." The deft song is called "If I Die 2nite."

Also on that CD is a song called I See "Death Around the Corner."

Born under the split astrological sign of Gemini, Pac was Icarus, far more than the media's favorite thug and around-the-way saint. With his poet's sensibility and gangsta façade, he was the angel who flew too close to the sun. Like the theater masks representing happiness and sadness tattooed on his back, Pac personified the duality of life, ying and yang, love and hate; he knew we must have hate to appreciate love, everything, as he said, is related at the core, everything is interdependent: "We may be different races, but we're all human, we all share the same emotions. We all respond to love and hate." A risk-taker by nature and nurture, the native New Yorker with the middle-weight's build had many questions that went unanswered before his wings were clipped by still unknown assailants. Pac's questions were as numerous as the ashes that his mother would later sprinkle over a tranquil hilltop in the City of Angels, the city Pac loved the most.

We had discussed these types of questions many times: "What is the best, most intelligent and adult way to manage life in America as an African-American man? Having grown up poor in Harlem and the Bronx, how do I peacefully turn the tables on the forces of oppression without being a sellout? Are there any other choices beside Field Nigger and House Nigger? How can I use my talent, honor my manhood and not get shot by the cops? They say I act like a thug when I try to protect what's mine, but in another place and time, would I have been fine, considered a courageous pharaoh or a genius? Where do I go to stay of out trouble? There's no a place called Careful USA. "Somebody tell me where to go from here/Cuz even thugs cry/ But does the Lord hear?'"

W.E.B. DuBois knew well what we went through in 1695 and 1965 and today. He knew well Pac's trial by fire. In *The Souls of Black Folk* DuBois wrote: "One ever feels his twoness—an American, a Negro . . . two warring ideals in one dark body." This Gemini had read both DuBois and Shakespeare's bloody tale of the warrior general, *Titus Andronicus*, and concurred.

Being a thug or gangsta was the 25-year-old's seemingly immature and half-conscious response to a ruling class that perpetuates its identity by commoditizing (marketing) black criminals and invisible/nonthreatening blacks (read Willie Horton and Bill Cosby). Pac morphed from a kinder and gentler poet of the '80s, into the '90s version of the graphic plantation stereotype, replete with handkerchief head (much to the chagrin of his bourgie fans—see Shaker Heights and Sag Harbor, Long Island). He played the thug/field nigger role because he related to the thugs he knew growing up, the only male role models that had shown him love and support for his dreams. The thug role was also profitable. He needed the money and he did not know how to maintain "the man that my mother raised me to be." But to become his mother's ideal would have been too one dimensional. The Gemini embraced his duality and seeming contradictions wholeheartedly. There was no real confusion on his part. He had to attack crooked cops because that's what warriors do, and he had to be a ladies man because that's what poets do. I was the one who was confused by my boy. I thought I could stop him from his mission of making war all out. In this light, it's easier to understand how this Gemini could make records that are polar opposites, like "Fuck the Police" and "Can U Get Away," "I Don't Give a Fuck" and "Keep Ya Head Up." I had just not seen anyone throw it down so hard in my generation. Who was the last person on the national stage who walked it like he talked it? Muhammad Ali? Malcolm X? I kept thinking that Pac needed to chill and get some anger management counseling.

His rap was, "The industrial revolution would not have happened without black inventions, but they don't want people to know that, because then Americans would have one more reason to respect black people, and black people would have one more reason to feel good about themselves. Ronald Reagan thinks everyone in America can get food, but they're just not looking hard enough. Bush made it three strikes and you're out. Clinton quietly made it one strike and you're out. Clinton passed an anti-terrorism bill that's repealing Americans' civil liberties based on a fear that the CIA helped create and you don't even know it, you're too busy wondering who's going to make it to the Superbowl—and I'm the problem? Nigga please."

Pac told me straight up no chaser: "I might get shot tomorrow Ses, but niggas like you die a little everyday. Everyday you peep game and don't do shit about it. Everyday you look at local and global oppression and don't do nothing about it, you die a little bit, your soul dies a little bit. Where we live and places like it are occupied territories. The racial composition of prisons. The use of prisoners as capitalist tools. The death rate of young black males, and black males in Harlem—shit in Harlem is worse than in the streets of Bangladesh—the increasing incarceration of women in general and black women in particular...Peep game, peep the game of life: jails are big business. Jails feed whole communities. Look at the three strikes law, in prison they over-charge you for telephone calls, they charge you for disciplinary problems, you do dangerous toxic work for corporations. But if there are no criminals, there is no income. Over the last 12 years, 71% of all new inmates were Black or Latino. Peep game. Prisons are growing exponentially. So we need to start figuring out another way out. And if you peep the game of life, you can see the guns are being turned away from Iran and Russia and North Korea and they're being turned at us. One of those guns is crack. It did what centuries of slavery couldn't do to the black family and at the same time, it sold a pipe-dream to young males of color that they could get rich quick, when all it did was kill thugs quickly on the streets or kill thugs slowly in prisons by sending them to jail for much longer sentences. So we are the prime target for all of America's guns and powerful resources. So if you're in the game, buy legit businesses, make them profitable, become elected officials. That's the power. That's a real gang that controls our communities, that controls the cops that oppress our communities, because right now we pay taxes for cops who oppress our communities and who are also on the take, so they get paid twice by the people they oppress. We're in a war and we're losing badly! We need every brother and sister to be strapped mentally!" Pac always kept it real and if you didn't like it you could step.

Perhaps Treach from the rap group Naughty by Nature said it best: "Pac didn't tell you what you needed to hear. He told you what you needed to know." If Pac had lived longer or had a father, he might have learned to temper his brutal honesty with sensitivity to others' feelings, putting himself in their place before speaking. He might have learned to balance the negative and positives in his life. But he wasn't meant to live very long. He was meant to be our wake up call.   "Bust this shit, Ses: these motherfuckas in government think they running slick shit we can't see. But we been peeped out their shit. The niggas they hire as Treasury secretaries and in senior treasury positions all come from Wall Street and multinational corporations, so the policies that they write that become laws, who do you think they are hooking up? And when they leave Washington after four years or whatever, who do you think is going to hook them up with an even phatter job than they had before they left? Feel me? The bottom line of the dot com bullshit in the late 1990s is one of the greatest financial manipulations and vic'ing of Americans of all colors in history. So bus' it: The head of the treasury department was head of a powerful Wall Street investment bank when he took the job at Treasury. His replacement at the bank was a dude who is now a Senator. This same bank is being sued in a variety of civil cases which occurred during the senator's watch when he was president of the bank, because his bank and other banks, during the whole dot com, dot bomb craze, manipulated Internet stocks on the day the stocks were offered to the public. The banks traded the shares back and forth to drive the prices of the Internet stocks from $15 to over $100 on the first day of trading. So they suckered the regular people into buying worthless Internet stocks. The end result was that the Treasury department got fat tax receipts in the short term because everybody was buying these stocks like crazy. Fuck the fact the business plans of half the companies didn't make sense. The head of Treasury, the same former head of the bank, was supposed to be protecting the public from this type of rip-off. The head of the Treasury department, as the man overseeing the IRS, was supposed to be watching out for crooked companies. But Clinton's homeboy at Treasury was like, yo, 'Those my niggas at Enron, Worldcom, HealthSouth, Global Crossing, Tyco, so chill on the fact that they cost investors and taxpayers billions with their false accounting schemes and ripped off millions in people's hard-earned retirement savings and then got golden exit packages when the companies closed, because the schemes were exposed.

"Meanwhile, all those employees are now out of work and no one wants to hire them because they have the taint of illegality on them. Meanwhile, the head nigga at Treasury, the former head of the bank, is like, the heads of those crooked companies are going to get a slap on the wrist—if that—because those are the niggas I be golfing with, and what am I gonna do, golf by myself? Ha ha ha! Am I right Bubba? Sure you're right, Bob.' And that's just the way shit goes in the Washington Beltway, yo. But you'll never see those whiteboys' faces on the cover of your newspapers. But I'll be plastered on there in a minute. I'm the problem. Meanwhile, these whiteboys are ripping off all of America like we blind. Peep game... The head of Treasury had oversight of the IRS but failed to deal with Islamic terror groups raising money in the United States. The head of Treasury used stock-market-crash protection schemes that kept the stock market/Internet bubble afloat by buying NASDAQ futures in Asia overnight to keep the US market propped up and tax revenues from stock investing soaring. The plan worked until 2000, the last year of the Clinton administration, when the NASDAQ started to plunge and lost half its value. The head of Treasury was running one of the largest financial bubbles in global history, which rocked the shit out of Americans of all colors, but it made "Bubba" Clinton look good for a few years. Aside from running his own games with the IRS, the head of Treasury, Robert Rubin, was using the IRS to investigate Clinton's enemies and, this is no joke, bailing out large US banks, aka his homies' investments in Mexico, Russia and Asia...But some brother is always on the cover the news? The only thing the head of Treasury and the media is doing is giving you a place to put your anger. Hate the black man. He's your enemy. Divide and conquer. Distract and destroy. I'm saying again—peep game, yo—get your paper, get your degrees, get real estate income, buy legit businesses, get into politics. That's where the real power is!"

For Pac, "Thug Life" meant facing "all challenges riding, mounted, face against the wind," to quote one of his favorite poets, Emily Dickinson. It meant, against all odds, walking with your head up, your chest out, proud to be "Black." Pac once told me, "A lot of these people who don't listen to all my music got it wrong. My music doesn't celebrate any type of image. My music is spiritual." You might ask how music that tells former vice president Dan Quayle to "eat a dick" can be spiritual. It is the spirit of resistance, the spirit of the undefeated. "Each day we are being wiped out, one by one. In Africa and in the U.S. Think of me as Bob Marley reborn, with a Glok. 'I love it when they fear me!/Holla if you hear me!'" There was no use trying to save this buffalo solider from what we may have considered as drowning. Was there a better way to do things, like not physically attacking the Hughes brothers because the directors dropped him from a film in an unprofessional manner? Yes, but violence was part of what he was sent here to do. His homegirl, Lisa "Left Eye" Lopes (R.I.P.) of R&B group TLC said: "Pac believed he was here on a mission. And he believed we wouldn't listen, but he had to do what he had to do."

When you heard Pac rap, you felt this immense power and passion in his voice. His revolutionary identity was repackaged and marketed as a gangsta identity. This thug identity, however, appeared to give him little leverage in the war between America's wealthy and poor. It gave him guns, drugs and convenient women. It was a fatal role many less celebrated black men have been fit into since slavery. As Baldwin wrote: "There exists among the intolerably degraded the perverse and powerful desire to force into the arena of the actual those fantastic crimes of which they have been accused, achieving their vengeance and their own destruction through making the nightmare real." Pac's nightmares were of being gunned down by corrupt cops.

Some gangsta rap fans challenged Shakur's persona, and his macho: the "street cred," right to assert hardcore lyrics. They viewed his pretty-boy looks and long eyelashes as soft. On the D train in New York once, a guy who was much bigger and harder looking than Pac, gave him a homicidal stare, like, "You punk, I should just kill you for the fuck of it." Pac's almond-shaped eyes narrowed to cobra slits, his malt-colored pupils fired, enraged. Pac's jacket was already off and he was charging toward the cat. I tackled Pac before he got to the dude. The guy looked straight ahead, trying to play it off. I told Pac, "Some stupid shit you let drop! Ah-ight!"

Another time, in Cali, certain gang members talked shit about the size of Shakur's heart. Pac strapped on his bullet proof vest, slapped long clips into rubber grips, and went to the gang-bangers' crib. He was set to let his Gloks pop—and didn't want to hear shit else. All he said was, "You ridin'?"

Pac walked in the door, cooly put his big heavy guns on the glass coffee table and lit a cigarette. "Yo," he said, "I heard y'all saying some shit. W's up?" One of the three guys there spoke for the group, "I don't know what you talking about Pac. Not me, Kid. You know how rumor be, Pac. . . ."

What struck me the most about Pac was his mind. He was amazingly intelligent and quick. He had a photographic memory and could recite lines of Shakespeare as easily as lines of Scarface. What struck his boy "Tyse" (Boxer Mike Tyson) about him was something much different: "God judges our heart. Men judge our actions. And that's what I thought was very special and genuine about him, and separated him from the majority of people in his field. Tupac would give you $1,000 if it was his last $1,000—boom—you got it. Most people are well behaved but not good. He wasn't well behaved, but he was good."

Pac had written and visited Tyson while Tyse was in prison. Pac would never forgot that Mike had gotten him and his crew of about 50 homeboys into a club in L.A. when he was 18.

Pac's road manager, Charles Fuller, explained in the *New Yorker* that "Pac felt, 'I have to prove that I'm hard.' I would say to Pac, 'Most gangsters are people who wish they didn't have to be hard.'" Pac felt that he had to take on all comers—the Hughes brothers, the racist crooked cops, the nazis, the illuminati (the original one-world government group that wants to enslave 95% of the world, many would say that the European union is just the first of many steps in that direction)—anybody who wanted to step up and get their head cracked open for fucking with one of his Kemetian queens and the N.I.G.G.A.Z who were here first and will be here last.

On Pac's back was a tattoo in script that read "Fuck the World." On the song of the same name he shouts: "Police call me rapist/You devils are so two-faceted/Want to see me locked in chains/Dropped in shame/Getting stopped by these crooked cops/Told the judge I'm in danger/That's why I had that .4-5 with one in the chamber/Label me a menace/ because I'm sitting here sipping on Guinness/Fuck the world!/Woke up screaming fuck the world!" Below that tattoo was an Ethiopian cross. Ethiopia was the only country in Africa not colonized. It is the country revered by rastafarians like Bob Marley. Inside the cross is the word *Exodus*, the famous Marley song that tells about a movement of God's, or Jah's, people: "We're the generation/who trod thru great tribulation/Jah come to breakdown downpression, rule equality/wipe away transgression/and set the captives free/we know where we're going/we know where we're from/we're leaving babylon/into our father's land/move, move, move, movement of jah people."

Pac: "Most of these dudes out here are actin'... let's start a revolution. Let's start out own country."

According to Fuller, the crescent-sloped "50 NIGGAAZ" tattoo above Pac's underwear-model abs (the "I" is a bullet), represents Pac's idea for black solidarity among the 50 states. And "nigga" for Shakur meant "Never Ignorant Getting Goals Accomplished. . . . We're going to take the word that they used and turn it around on them . . . to make it positive."

His childhood friend and manager, Watani Tyehimba, defined the "THUG LIFE" tattoo across his stomach: "The Hate That U Gave Little Niggaz—Fuck Everyone." Pac wanted to make sure he never forgot the dispossessed, the oppressed, never forgot where he came from. He was straddling two worlds and looking for answers. This was his internal struggle. He saw that we rarely make it as black people unless we sellout. He was saying he never would."

I was on the other end of the spectrum telling him, "N.I.G.G.A.Z" in corporate America, who are well educated, or who run their own businesses in competitive industries don't sellout. They battle against overt and covert racism daily. He never had a father to teach him how to get to that level or how to fight those battles, and his mother, a former Black Panther, couldn't teach him how to be man. Gemini or not, he had no father-figure to teach him how to maintain his mother's core values. Yet he made a firm and permanent stand for his angelic beliefs, like gospel singer Kirk Franklin, who had learned to be a man from his holy Father, and Claude Brown, who had learned how to be a man from his mentor, as Brown described in his autobiography *Manchild in the Promise Land*. But there was no adult male to show Pac how to harmoniously balance the inner conflict between the id and the superego, how to collect on the rich spiritual inheritance of his Kemetian manhood. So he was just playing the game, the game of life, and doing what he was supposed to be doing: rep'ing ebony warriors while showing leadership and love to black people, but you would have only understood that if you heard all of the man's music and read or listened to all of his views. The media was not going to portray him as anything approaching leadership status or as an intellectual. His friends couldn't help him get to the next level of his development, because it was a spiritual level. His friends Suge Knight and Mike Tyson were portrayed in the media as wealthy and ignorant. For many, Knight, a 6' 5", 315-pound former member of the notorious Bloods gang, symbolized flash and violent authority in the music industry. He has since served nine years for assault and probation violation after Pac's death. Mike "Mad Dog" Tyson served several years for "rape" and was suspended for one year from boxing for biting his opponent's ear when he was out boxed and losing his championship crown.

Pac and I grew up watching "New York's finest" get away with crimes like rape and murder, much like the police massacre of the unarmed Amadou Diallo (R.I.P.). Once, when we were eleven, we went into the local record store to see undercover cops smashing the glass record cases with bats in demand of their protection money. Numerous police examples like these colored our early perceptions of right, wrong and justice.

When my brothers and sisters and I would mess up repeatedly, my Jamaican father would say, "Those who can't hear must feel," and get the belt. Pac felt America had messed up repeatedly and would not hear the cries of the oppressed, so it was critical to speak the only language those in power seemed to know.

In 1993, Shakur was arrested for shooting two off-duty Atlanta policemen. He claimed he intervened when he saw them bullying a black driver and that the cops drew their guns first. Authorities stated three facts: the officers were at fault, they had alcohol in their systems and one of the guns used to menace Shakur was stolen from an evidence locker. All charges against the shooting star were dismissed. It helped that black music executives in Atlanta (for example, executives of LaFace Records) had a lot of juice/power at that time.

In 1995, Shakur was sentenced to a maximum of four and a half years—ostensibly for touching Ms. Ayanna Jackson's rear. (Pac on the bust: "The powers that be always try to discredit black men as rapists and sexual deviants to weaken our credibility in the black community; the shit's on page one of the Counter Intelligence Program, COINTELPRO, manual").

Legal experts agree that it was an unusually lengthy sentence for the crime committed, especially in light of the fact that he was sentenced to a maximum-security prison. When Pac stood up to hear the sentence from the judge, the judge asked him if he had anything to say. The courtroom became as quiet as a funeral mass. Pac said, "It doesn't matter what you do to me now. You could give me a hundred years. It don't matter. I'm in God's hands now."

During the trial, the female prosecutor had railed about Shakur being a "thug." Some experts think that alone was grounds for a new trial. Bail was set at $3 million, another curious, and many legal experts say, unfair decision meant to chill the latest icon of black liberation. Pac said, "People get it twisted. They think I talk about bitches and hoes and I'm talking about all women. That's not the case. There are certain women who are bitches, gold diggers, whatever, and that's who I'm talking about. These women are no stranger to good women, who do call these types of women 'bitches.'" He explained it in a narrative and in more detail on "Wonda Why They Call U B." How he feels about good women can be heard on "White Man's World."

Pac claimed that four days before the incident leading to his arrest, Ms. Jackson had fellated him in a secluded area of the New York nightclub Nell's; and later that night they had gone back to his hotel and had intercourse. After that initial interlude, Ms. Jackson had left several messages for him that were unreturned.

Shakur testified that when Ms. Jackson, age 19, came to visit him at his hotel suite for a second time, they had watched television in the living room with three of his associates. Then he and Jackson went into the bedroom. Shortly thereafter, his three associates entered the room and he left.

Ms. Jackson said she was undressed, grabbed at from behind, held, and forced to perform oral sex on Shakur and another man: music-industry insider Jacques Agnant's friend "Tim." It was "Tim" who had introduced Ms. Jackson to Shakur at Nell's four nights earlier. "Tim" left the hotel before the police arrived and was never arrested.

On the witness stand, Ms. Jackson explained that after the assault, she exited the room crying, but Agnant told her sarcastically to "chill," because he "would hate to see what happened to [Shakur's friend] Mike Tyson happen to Tupac," meaning a woman charging Shakur with rape. Ms. Jackson called hotel security.

Agnant's lawyer, a friend of the NYPD's Patrolmen's Benevolence Association, has reportedly maintained that the case against Shakur was "very weak," yet he couldn't find one cop with a good thing to say about Shakur. Agnant was charged with two misdemeanors and released. His indictment was dropped.

Pac acknowledged that "even though I'm innocent of the charge they gave me, I'm not innocent in terms of the way I was acting. . . . I'm just as guilty for not doing nothing as I am for doing things . . . I know I feel ashamed—because I wanted to be accepted and because I didn't want harm done to me, I didn't say nothing."

Shakur wrote about Agnant on his final album: "I hope my true muthafukas know/This be the realest shit I ever wrote /Listen while I take you back/and lace this track/A real live tale/About a snitch named Haitian Jack/Knew he was working for the Feds/Set me up/Wet me up/Nigga stuck me up."

Shakur's boy, Mike Tyson, had earlier warned him about Agnant possibly being a Federal informant. The last verse refers to Shakur's belief that Agnant was behind him being shot the first time: When Shakur went to earn some much needed money for legal fees by rapping on a Little Shawn track at a Times Square recording studio, three guys followed him and his crew into the lobby, whipped out automatic weapons and shouted, "Don't nobody move! Everybody on the floor!" By the time Pac pulled his .45, the men had already shot him five times.

"I couldn't hear nothing," Shakur would say later. "And I couldn't see nothing; it was all just white."

The dudes popped off Shakur's bloody gold and jet. No one was arrested in connection with the robbery and attempted homicide. Although Shakur had read Malcolm X's biography, up until then he never thought Black people would try to harm him.

When Shakur, then 23, returned to court for the first time after the Times Square shooting, he was wrapped in white bandages from head to toe. This is how his biological father had seen him for the first time, dressed like a mummy, in the hospital. What did his father say to him about his troubles, or his nonexistence during Pac's childhood? That day in the hospital room his father cried loudly and praised God that his son was alive. He vowed to Pac that he would be there for him from now on. He promised Pac he would call him day and night. He would do better, but truly, he had had a far worse childhood than Pac, and had never known his own father. Pac's biological father did not ask for money.

At the Jackson trial, Pac was wheeled into the courtroom with one leg raised in a cast. He again looked like a mummy who'd collided with a Mack truck.

Connie Bruck, reporting in the *New Yorker* on "The Takedown of Tupac Shakur," writes that "Iris Crews, one of his many attorneys in the Ms. Jackson sex-abuse case—had been leery about representing Tupac, but became beguiled and devoted ("Had he been this foul-mouthed, woman-hating kid, I wouldn't have done it"). Crews recalled that one day, as he sat in court with a bunch of young children climbing all over him during a recess, he had remarked to her, "'If I don't work, these kids [family members' children] don't eat.' Crews explained that 'He'd been deprived of his childhood, and then, at twenty, he had twenty people to support.'"

Beyond supporting children that weren't his, he had enormous legal fees for cases all over the country. After nearly six months in prison [for the sex-abuse case], despite the money being advanced by Interscope [his first lawsuit-plagued label], Tupac's funds were depleted."

After Shakur's four platinum albums, there was no money to fund the chain of daycare centers that the crossover artist wanted to build for working mothers like his own, no capital to underwrite the youth center for oppressed teens, and no "cheddar" to establish the 800 number, so kids could call him if they had a problem and wanted to talk. There was, mysteriously, no money for any of his numerous angelic plans. His mother Alfeni is executing his estate and attempting to sort the murky financial facts.

After growing up poor in the Bronx and Harlem with his mother, a celebrated Black Panther from the '70s, Pac moved to Baltimore and more poverty as a teen. In a 1995 deposition, Pac stated that in Maryland, "We didn't have any lights. I used to sit outside by the street lamps and read *The Autobiography of Malcolm X*. And it made it so real to me that I didn't have any lights at home and I was sitting outside on the benches reading this book. And it changed me, it moved me. And then of course my mother had books by people like . . . Patrice Lumumba and Stokely Carmichael, *Seize the Time* by Bobby Seale and *Soledad Brother* by George Jackson. And she would tell these stories of things that she did or she saw or she was involved with, and it made me feel a part of something. She always raised me to think that I was the Black Prince of the revolution. . . . In my family, every black male with the last name of Shakur that ever passed the age of 15 has either been killed or put in jail. There are no Shakurs, black male Shakurs, out right now, free, breathing, without bullet holes in them or cuffs on his hands. None."

In Baltimore, Pac's life took a critical turn. Accepted into the acclaimed Baltimore School for the Arts after his mother's relentless lobbying, the specialized high school for the performing and fine arts became his savior and sanctuary, the home where Pac felt the freest, and finally, at 14, like he belonged.

"For a kid from the ghetto, the Baltimore School for the Arts is Heaven . . . I learned ballet, poetry, jazz, music, everything, Shakespeare, acting, everything as well as academics. . . . I was the mouse king in the *Nutcracker*. . . . I was an artist." The only gangs he was involved with were "Shakespeare gangs." At BSA he met the "omega of his heart," true and dear friend, actress Jada Pinkett. Strength had recognized strength. Game had recognized game.

But home became increasingly intense. "My mother was pregnant, on dope," Shakur recalls in the deposition, "dope crack. She had a boyfriend who was violent toward her. We weren't staying in our spot. We were staying in someone else's spot. We never could pay the rent. She always had to sweet-talk this old white man that was the landlord into letting us [stay] for another month. And he was making passes at my mom. So I didn't want to be there anymore. So I sacrificed my future in the School of the Arts to get on a bus [at age 16] to go cross country to California with no money" to live in an oppressed community north of San Francisco called Marin City, with the wife of jailed Black Panther "Geronimo" Pratt, my godfather.

But life by the Bay was anything but cool. Kids called the skinny Tupac "Tube Sock," and "Tuberculosis."

"I didn't fit in. I was the outsider. . . . I dressed like a hippie, they teased me all the time. I couldn't play basketball, I didn't know who the basketball players were. . . . I was the target for gangs. They used to jump me, things like that. . . . I thought I was weird because I was writing poetry and I hated myself, I used to keep it a secret. . . . I was really a nerd." The welcoming committee to Oakland were two cops who beat him down for jaywalking—"Know your place nigga!" They introduced his face to the concrete several times and took him in for resisting arrest, because he protested being hassled like was in 1980s South Africa. He sued the police for that false arrest and won $42,000. The incident left him with mental and physical scars he would never forgive or forget.

Marin City is not to be confused with Marin, which sits above Marin City, nestled in lush greenery amid multimillion dollar homes. The residents of Marin can literally look down upon the poor of Marin City, where there is no grocery store, only a liquor store.

On his first album, 1991's revolutionary *2pacalypse Now*, Shakur boldly dramatized violence between racist police officers and young black men. Shakur says in the deposition that he isn't a proponent of violence toward the police, he's only telling tales about racial profiling and life in poor urban areas: narratives that often end with young black men going to jail or dying. "Before you can understand what I mean, you have to know how I lived or the how the people I'm talking to live. . . . You don't have to agree with me, but just to understand what I'm talking about. Compassion, to show compassion."

Pac considered his songs allegories of life in America. "My lyrics are about struggling and overcoming." Pac felt that we have to regain control of our communities and regulate whatever illegal activities must take place within them, so there could be, at the bare minimum, safe zones for kids. For those who feel that they have to live as gangsters, Pac said: "Now, if we do want to live a thug life, and a gangsta life, and all a that, OK, so stop being cowards and let's have a revolution. But we don't want to do that. Dudes just want to live a character, they want to be cartoons. But if they really wanted to do something, if they was that tough, alright, let's start our own country, let's start a revolution, let's get outta here, let's do something. It's way past time for the freedom to walk on any street without being treated like slaves by cops. And it's damn sure way past time for jobs with wages that can cover basic cost of living. And if I can't live free, if I can't live with the same respect as the next man, I don't want to be here."

His first movie, 1992's *Juice* (slang for *power*), introduced his charismatic screen presence, seductive eyes, and ferocious nature. He played Bishop, a son who resorts to crime when his father can no longer support the family. The irreverent Bishop's becomes a homicidal psychotic who falls from a building to his death in the film's climax, a la Icarus. In an earlier scene, Bishop shoots a teen rival point blank in an alley and then shouts where he's from—"Uptown mutha-fucka!"—at the dead young man before stomping away in his black boots. After making the film,

Shakur told MTV: "I didn't have a father and that makes me cold and bitter." He was able to tap the emptiness as a source of rage, but he also knew that: "I can slip into any role, because at the end of the day, I know I can look in the mirror and see my soul."

Yet the day Shakur spoke with his biological, ex-Black Panther Billy Garland, while recovering from five gun shot wounds to the head, hand and groin suffered in the Times Square shooting, he was happy to see him, albeit insult to injury. I couldn't believe Garland's audacity, and told Pac that when I visited him. Pac, with uncommon grace, said, "Hey, he's still my father. He was never there for me, true, but that don't mean . . ." The shooting had diminished his body but made him huge. He had always believed that he would one day meet his father, but now he had love to balance the hate he felt for his biological. "Faith," Pac said, "maybe it's like Baldwin said, it's 'the evidence of things not seen.'"

That day, I told him my three best jokes, and he and his roommate laughed at the last one. It was good to see him getting better. He could be very funny. We used to crack up and snap on people all the time. I remember once, I went to visit him when he was on tour. He clowned around in the dressing room, doing a Rick James impersonation, wearing the long black wig and all—singing, "Temptations sing! Superfreak, superfreak!" After the jokes, three doctors came in and talked to him about the second operation on his hand, which they were going to perform in the morning. He was, surprisingly, his usual talkative and intellectual self; his mind was as quick-witted and agile as ever, as if he had vowed not to go yet, or to go out fighting. He told me he was aching to get his full strength back, work on a new album, take more acting classes, go on the previously planned tour spanning Egypt, Ghana, Senegal, Kenya, Nigeria and South Africa. I hung with him for three hours. I hadn't planned to stay that long because I wanted him to rest, but he had a lot to say. He told me about a film project he was excited about. He'd be working with the young *Boyz in the Hood* director, the youngest person ever to be nominated for a directing Oscar. Pac said Singleton was a "hot shot," and all I could do was smile, because that's how a lot of suits characterized Pac: "He's an arrogant young hot shot with a bad temper, a loud mouth—but a great fucking talent." The project Singleton wanted him for was the 1993 film *Poetic Justice*, a love story. He would play a young man from an oppressed community in Los Angeles trying to do the right thing, get his life on track. In the film, his character meets a girl who challenges him to strive for his goals, and he does.

In both *Juice* and *Justice*, he garnered critical acclaim for his impressive acting talent and animal magnetism. In both, he displayed a child-like vulnerability and a take-no-bullshit attitude. This Gemini had to succeed in both movies and music. In the 1997 movie *Gridlock'd*, he played a drug addict who tries to quit after his girlfriend overdoses. *Gridlock'd* showcased Pac's ability to pull from within himself whatever he needed to make the character believable and engaging. Whether it was bad-boy allure or the humanization of a career addict, Pac's strength lay in adding depth and dimensions to a character, regardless of how poorly the character was written or how badly the movie was made. 1997's low-budget *Gang Related* starred Pac as a crooked cop, who viewers couldn't turn away from because of the intensity of his performance. Pac worked extremely hard on his crafts. He wrote quickly and had a work ethic second to none in hip hop. Always in the studio, he recorded over 200 songs in his brief professional career.

At the time of his death, his record "How Do You Want It?" was the number 10 single in America. In all, he sold over

10 million albums and more than 33 million records. He died with less than $100,000 in the bank. Death Row owed Pac $4 to $9 million at the time of his death. Pac's mother is suing to get the publishing rights—the masters—to the 200 songs Pac wrote. Pac liked to say, "I write about raw human needs." His lyrics could be feminist and understanding on one track, yet rude and violent on another. His velvety voice matured from a sophomoric tenor to a gravelly bass. His unmistakable staccato intonation sounded like a clip being set off ("Ballad of a Dead Souljah" is emblematic of his spit-fire delivery). His signature voice could be simultaneously menacing, heart-wrenching and thought-provoking. And on some records, he could clown with the best of them, as in the "Humpty" video with Digital Underground (the fun-rap group that gave him his start as a back-up dancer) and on his hilltop-mansion video farce, "I Get Around," where beautiful girls in bikinis chased him from Jacuzzis to bedrooms.

"It's just a fun game . . . the game of life," Pac said while working on a video for his last album, which showed him dying in an ambulance from gun shot wounds. "I know one day they're gonna shut the game down, but I gotta go around the board as many times as I can before it's my turn to leave."

The poignancy of early smash songs like "Part-Time Mutha" and "Brenda's Got a Baby" heralded the arrival of an evocative griot of poor African-American life. "Brenda" is a haunting and powerful song about a 12-year-old girl who is raped by her cousin and then throws the resulting baby in a dumpster. It led Pac to say that "when this song came out, no male rappers at all—anywhere, were talking about problems that females were having, number one. Number two, it talked about sexual abuse, it talked about child molestation, it talked about the effects of poverty, it talked about how one person's problems can affect a whole community of people. It talked about drugs, the abuse of drugs, broken families . . . how she couldn't leave the baby, you know, the bond the mother has with her baby and how . . . women need to be able to make a choice."

The problem with not listening to all of his music and understanding his political philosophy is that the seemingly chameleon-like attitude distilled by the media cheapens the sentiment of his songs and his credibility. We Americans like our good guys true blue, and our bad guys truly evil—no humanity, no constant state of flux, no I'm still finding myself at 25, no I'm still searching for my soulmate, or twin, to make myself complete. Such clear labeling enables us to know who is who, with little mental exercise, although we widely acknowledge that most U.S. males don't reach manhood until they're at least 27; and since World War II that age of responsibility has risen, with some never achieving it, oddly enough, in this age of instant gratification.

In light of this, it's easier to understand why Pac dedicated the following poem to himself:

I exist in the depths of solitude
pondering my true goal
Trying 2 find peace of mind
and still preserve my soul
CONSTANTLY yearning 2 be accepted
And from all receive respect
Never compromising but sometimes risky
and that is my only regret
A young heart with an old soul
how can there be peace
how can I be in the depths of solitude
when there R 2 inside of me
This Duo within me causes

The perfect opportunity
2 learn and live twice as fast
as those who accept simplicity
   "In the Depths of Solitude"

After recording 1995's *Me Against the World*, Pac explained to writer Kevin Powell that now "I can be free. When you do rap albums, you got to train yourself. You got to constantly be in character. You used to see rappers talking all that hard shit, and then you see them in suits at the American Music Awards. I didn't want to be that type of nigga. I wanted to keep it real, and that's what I thought I was doing. But. . . . let somebody else represent it [thug life]. I represented it too much. I was thug life." Pac felt that he diagnosed "T.h.u.g. L.i.f.e." the way a doctor diagnosed a disease, giving us information on it as well as a cure, if we wished to take it.

Pac's keep ya head up, get legit, get into politics, "T.h.u.g. L.i.f.e." stance was only the latest chapter of a music book that started in the mid-1970s. Rap "blew up" in 1979 with the feel-good song, "Rapper's Delight" by the Sugar Hill Gang. Previously, rap had strictly been an urban (and New York-centered) phenomenon filled with funny false bravado and hyperbolic tales of Romeos' prowess (the best and funniest at this was Spoony G back in the days of the 8-track tape). If there was a rivalry between two rappers (like the one between the two Roxannes in the early '80s), no matter how hard-edged and hyped, listeners knew it was for fun and profit, not to be taken seriously. In the mid-80s, groups like Run-DMC (with their party-funk sound) and De La Soul (with their laid-back, neo-hippie vibe) brought more frenetic beats and different styles of rhyming to the game, which was still dominated by "old school" four-count beats. These two groups expanded the genre to new commercial

heights, extending rap's influence into fashion and the mainstream like no one—except rap impresario Russell Simmons—
had ever imagined. With the subsequent ascent of conscious,
political and "Keep it Real" groups like Public Enemy (who
easily met their goal of "reach[ing] the bourgeois and rock[ing]
the boulevard!") and the street-raw N.W.A. (Niggers With Attitude) from Compton, Cali, the same demographic that had
given America blues, bebop (slang for *fighting*) and rock, had now
given it hip hop.

DJ Marley Marl would soon bring fresh loops to hip hop.
Rob Base would later speed up the pace with the eternal club
fave "It takes 2," and Big Pun (R.I.P., yo) would eventually put
down that distinctive South Bronx flavor for the "ghetto bru-
nettes," *boricuas* (Puerto Ricans) and *morenos* (Latinos with dark
skin).

But before those three, gangsta rap would emerge in the
celebrated form of three West Coast MCs—Ice-T (whose anti-
police brutality song, "Cop Killer," ignited a firestorm of controversy), Dr. Dre (the first producer to make rap songs melodic)
and Too Short (the pioneer of pimp lyrics and funk beats). The
marketing for the genre would become much like the pit bulls
seen in almost every gangsta-rap video thereafter—ferocious.
And that dangerous dog found a home with white males, who
accounted for approximately 70 percent of gangsta rap sales.
Many of these males enjoyed the vicarious thrills from their safe
suburban houses. Like many young males, they were searching
for role models to teach them how to be strong and rugged.
The misogyny was only part and parcel of an aesthetic acted
out earlier by Jimmy Cagney and Humphrey Bogart's gangster
characters: slapping your woman around was nothing new in
the dialectic of popular American culture. You had to show her
who was boss, and as many of these consumers believed, every

woman secretly loves a brute. Maybe the challenge is for "nice guys" to viciously beat the brute's ass?

Perhaps the music industry is as Will Smith (a.k.a. fun-rapper the Fresh Prince), describes: "Get everything you can as fast as you can get it, and fuck everybody."

Born Lesane Parish Crooks, Shakur's mother Alfeni has reportedly said Tupac "was named after the last Incan chief to be tortured, brutalized and murdered by Spanish conquistadors . . . a warrior." When Pac made the "Holla If You Hear Me" video, whatever doubts the cops had about his position on crooked racist cops were clarified. "Holla" is, to date, the boldest anti-police brutality video ever made.

As the violent '90s rolled on, Pac wrote about death and the death of innocents more frequently. When his gun was used in the accidental death of 6-year-old Qa'id Walker-Teal, Pac was devastated. Pac's mourning would, unlike his tears, never cease. Like the main character in his favorite Shakespeare play *Macbeth*, Pac had supped full of blood and now saw Birnam Wood steadily approaching. In his poem titled "In the Event of My Demise," Pac wrote:

When my heart can beat no more
I hope I die for a principle or a belief
     that I have lived for
I will die before my time because
     I already feel the shadow's depth
So much I wanted to accomplish
     Before I reached my death

When the world lost Pac, it lost a portion of its soul. It lost a prodigy, an activist, a revolutionary, a prophet. God's black sheep, God's dark lamb, God's angry black ram.

Pac explained in a radio interview several weeks before sailing on that, "This is the life that they gave me. This is the life that I made. You know how they say, 'You made your bed now lay in it'? I tried to move. I can't move to no other bed. This is it." The sheet is stretched and the bed narrow, to quote Virginia Woolf.

For a Gemini like Shakur to move to another bed, to make a new life and to change his level of consciousness and spirituality, he perhaps had to first find his twin: his spiritual brother; or his soulmate: his earth.

The origin of the story about the search for the twin begins in ancient Egypt. The 3rd dynasty pharaoh Djozer ("pharaoh" means "the great/fertile house, abundant with children") had a great secretary of state who built the first pyramid, the step pyramid at Saqarra. (In Egypt, they say it is not a matter of building high, but building deep. When you visit Saqarra, I hope you feel the vibration of Imhotep's genius, because you will notice that there is an underground temple that goes down for at least three stories, built with what looks like poured concrete, and the only way down to those temples are via steps that are no more than three feet wide. The walls all the way down are seamless, again like poured concrete, built approximately 4,000 years B.C., with no rock quarries for miles, but I digress). The pyramid's architect, Imhotep, was also a physician and a scribe who wrote that two brothers were born from a loving union between the sun god Ra and a mortal of swan-like beauty, Leda. This "Tale of the Twins," known also as "The Way of the Gemini," maintains that the brothers' love for each other made them inseparable. They grew up to become great soldiers. When one was killed in battle, the other could not go on living, and he asked Ra to let him join his brother in Heaven.

Rap star Biggie Smalls, 25, was assassinated while waiting at a red light, execution-style. The drive-by shooting occurred shortly after Tupac's murder. Media reports maintain that Smalls was murdered as a result of a feud between West Coast rap (Shakur) and East Coast rap (Smalls). Critics of this notion (such as Smalls's mother) argue that the bicoastal feud theory is silly: These were two young black men unafraid of challenging authority, who had vast influence over other young black men and incarcerated men, and who consequently were killed by the same forces that assassinated Kennedy, divided and conquered the Black Panthers, and that still allow the KKK and white supremacy groups to operate. Allegedly, the FBI had both men under surveillance at the time of their deaths (Pac asserts this on his song, "Picture Me Rollin,") yet the homicide suspects' cars were lost in the ensuing chases. The only witnesses who could have identified the suspects were murdered. Orlando Anderson, who Shakur scuffled with earlier that evening, had no alibi, but he was never investigated by police. The police investigations in both cities were, by independent accounts, error-filled, and at best, sloppy. Las Vegas and the City of Angels, where Biggie Smalls was murdered, have deep triple K roots.

Whatever the reason for their deaths, the two Gemini were once great friends. Both were born in the borough of Kings, Brooklyn. Both were natural leaders and fighters: Shakur, as the prince of the rap revolution, and Biggie, as the godhead of hip hop. Pac had helped Biggie learn the game when Biggie was a rookie. Both were highly ambitious and incredibly talented; both wrote violent and loving lyrics; both were actors who could transform and adapt to new surroundings; both loved language and literature; both were highly intelligent and possessed the ability to deftly freestyle any situation; both loved spontaneity, luminous conversation, travel, the thrill of the chase, acting and adoring entourages. Both were charming and charismatic, living in a world of glittering parties and pyrotechnic concerts, shunning details in favor of creative chaos. Both served time in jail. Both loved the spotlight and working all night in the studio. Shakur allegedly knew Biggie's girlfriend, Faith, intimately. Both felt they would die before their last CDs were released (Biggie's first CD was *Ready to Die*, and like Pac, he made a video about being shot and going to heaven. One of Biggie's first records was "You're Nobody Till Someone Kills You"). In the City of Angels life had imitated art. In Vegas prophecy had become reality.

Pac, however, could not see that Biggie was his spiritual twin. He could only see him as, at least on his records, as a traitorous friend who was now only a jealous "fat mutha-fucka!," the "Notorious P.I.G." And this was perhaps, as Biggie's mother suggests, because of the same COINTELPRO-like misinformation used to divide and conquer the Black Panthers, i.e., "cultivating this big East Coast versus West Coast feud and perpetuating it in the media." When Biggie ran into Pac, he confronted Pac about all his trash talking. Pac's response: "I'm trying to sell records, B." He might as well as have said to Big: "It's not personal. It's just business, baby. Manipulating the media before they do it to us." Or, as Pac put it on the posthumous *Until the End of Time* CD, "They say we hate the East Coast/Well that's funny/We got a lot of love for any nigga gettin' money."

Controversy and conflict are always good for sales, as the Real Roxanne and Roxanne Shante had learned so well. This lesson was not lost on Pac, who had taught Biggie that you have to make radio-friendly records and but also hardcore tracks for your real fans.

Pac may not have recognized Biggie as his twin, but he immediately recognized his earth, Kadeisha Jones. She was the spiritual wife he had been searching for. After many romances, as well an early marriage with a sweet co-ed, Pac had finally found the twin that would make him whole and be his better half. Ms. Jones told me that when she first met Pac at a club she had thought, "He is so *cute!*" Shakur found in the daughter of (mega-music producer) Quincy Jones the woman who mirrored his consciousness, maturity, hunger for intellectual stimulation, and lust for life. He asked her to be his wife, and she gleefully accepted. Ms. Jones explained to me that her love for Pac was like the love writer Anais Nin felt for her man, as Ms. Nin described in her diary, *Fire: A Journal of Love*: "'Our talks are wonderful interplays, not duels but swift illuminations of one another. I can make his tentative thoughts click. He enlarges mine. I fire him. He makes me flow. There is always movement between us. And he is grasping. He takes hold of me like prey.'"

The Shining Serpent will now reside in the pantheon of our illusions, no doubt in discourse at this moment with fellow Gemini Billie Holiday, Marilyn Monroe (whom he dedicated a poem to: "The Star Within") and John F. Kennedy—all intelligent, vulnerable, Icarus—myths made real. Supernovas reflecting all too closely the tragic beauty of the American identity. As we enter the Age of Aquarius, the brotherhood of man, it is critical to remember these angels with dirty faces and their gifts to us in their short visits.

In the small hours of the seventh day, Shakur's body racked in its final moments on his hospital bed. One lung had already collapsed. Kadeisha clutched his hand as she forced back tears, because earlier he had asked her not to cry. Now, he said to her, "I, I can't breathe. . . ." She looked at the fire diminishing in his eyes and wished to God she was carrying his child! Her eyes pressed tight. She felt the sorrow growing deeper within her chest, a hollowing cavity of pain. She could not hold the tears back and squeezed his hand harder, as if hoping to transfer her life force into his. In the hallway, media reps circled his room negotiating the rights to straight-to-video movies about his life.

No arrests have been made in connection with his homicide or his brother Biggie's. Tupac Amaru Shakur is survived by his mother and sister. Christopher Wallace (Biggie Smalls) is survived by his mother. On one of the greatest hip-hop records of all time, "Juicy," Biggie Smalls penned the line: "Stereotypes of a black male misunderstood/but it's still all good."

When the innovative author who wrote the book, *Three Guineas*, a tome about resisting coercion and tyranny, later thought about the characters in her novel-in progress, *Mrs. Dalloway*, she wondered: "Why does someone have to die? Someone has to die in order that the rest of us should value life more. And who will die? The poet will die. The visionary."

Tupac Amaru Shakur, the man who embodied the contradictions of life: "Everything I do has to be for the love of Black people—my music, my acting, interviews, everything." He is the largest selling hip hop artist of all time. In January of 2005, his posthumously released CD, *Loyal to the Game*, debuted at number one on the Billboard charts. It was the third of his posthumous CDs to reach number one. Pac has sold 24 million albums, 18 million of which have come after his assassination.

Miles away, on the Zuni reservation in Southern California, gooey eggs emerge from a cobra's womb. The platinum-colored tip of the cobra's tail shakes as the last slick white egg slowly protrudes, spilling and wobbling in the dirt. The rattle sound is heard for miles in the night wind. The moon above is cratered, powdery, but strangely seductive...sexual. It seems covered with luminous white dust and snowy glitter. It glows warmly from within, throbbing lightly, like some living orb inching closer to Earth, as if for a long slow kiss. Its color is the same as the tip of the cobra's tail. One last egg squeezes forward, slips out and rocks back and forth awkwardly before remaining still...and then cracking open. A tiny head appears, and then another, both silver, luminescent. Their young black tongues hiss, spitting venom at the moon, sons of the dust tasting warm night air...

A noon tide have you been our twilight, and your youth has given us dreams to dream/No stranger are you among us, nor a guest, but our son and dearly beloved/Suffer not yet our eyes to hunger for your face. . . .

. . . Let not the waves of the sea separate us now, and the years you have spent in our midst become a memory/You have walked among us a spirit, and your shadow has been light upon our faces/Much have we loved you/But speechless was our love, and with veils has it been veiled/And ever has it been that love knows not its own depth until the hour of separation.

Kahil Gibran
The Prophet

For Siobhan

PROSE

10...Under the Heavens

I saw the vision there.

A transcendental error led to my Harlem team playing in Long Island's premier 16-and-under tournament rather than the nationals.

Sitting on the aluminum courtside bleachers with her crew of 16-year-old protégés, she looked 16. She gave the girls beaming up at her Venus envy.

I stomped up the bleachers, stopped right in front of her, and said, "Those sneakers are *on!*"

She giggled, as if to say, I know what you really like: these long tan stems. She was wrong.

She told me about the sneakers for 10 or 15 minutes, concluding with a coy smile, "Yeah, they rock!" I looked up at the pristine sky and then back into those bluest of eyes. My strongest muscle thumped, my mouth dried. I shook my head, not believing my luck.

I introduced myself and said, "This club is way too small. They really need to expand it."

She giggled again, because the place is the size of Puerto Rico.

"Come on," she said, "I'll give you the nickel tour of our little place."

We walked and talked before she watched me lose a close match to their No. 1 singles player.

In the snack bar, we sat at a round white enamel table, shaded by a blue and white umbrella. In between bites of rocky road, she told me about what she described as her "bor-ing" life of coaching, clam bakes, sun-bathing and trying to figure out her next move after recently graduating from a small Jesuit college in Connecticut, where she had majored in zoology before losing interest in med school and everything but tennis, which she'd played since she could walk. And she didn't want to stop the only positive constant, because then her whole world would crumble, but she didn't tell me that yet. You could tell she'd been playing since birth, because one honey-colored forearm was slightly larger than the other.

As we talked, we fell into a debate about "What is a pure truth?"

"The only pure truth is mathematics," she said. Like many Aries, she can be very strong, confident, direct, and a little bumptious. "It's the only universal language and it *can* be proven."

"Typical pre-med," I said, remembering my best friend Steve's sister, a former Howard U. zoology major now at Hopkins medical school. "Do you think Shakespeare, or any of the romantic poets, like Shelley or Keats, would add love?"

She paused for a long while before saying, in a dubious tone, ". . . Maybe."

Looking at her oval face, with its soft slopes, I realized that sometimes when you first meet someone, the knowledge that it isn't the first time transcends logic and reality. And the unexpected has already been felt. I wondered, as she looked at me intensely with her sapphire gems, could she see my anger, my fear, my strength? Had she seen them already?

"Do you," I asked, "think a person with predatory animal instincts can be trained to trust completely?"

"No!" she shot back. Steve's sister had said, "yes."

We continued talking at length about diverse topics: Islam and women, Mormons and marriage, the beautiful handling of fast cars, existentialism—the nature of freedom, responsibility, and the unexplainable in a Godless universe. As we talked, we unconsciously moved closer, drinking in each other's words, and faces, kissing mid-sentence. Our lips didn't want to part, but did so, out of propriety, with a slow sweet stickiness that reminded me of strawberry cotton candy. Her eyes shimmered, incandescent.

"*Wow*," she said, almost out of breath, falling back dizzily into her chair. "I feel like I'm going to faint." She pushed her hands through hair as golden as wine. After she caught her breath, she jolted forward and slapped my hand—"Stop making me swoon!" Smiling, she fell back against her seat just as suddenly, laughing, as if I was a humorous impostor: "Are you *sure* you're 16?"

I returned her warm smile. I had fallen marching up the bleachers.

"Hey, you're the one making *me* swoon," I said. I got the sense she didn't like to lose control. But that was my whole game. I like to see what's at the core. I believe in strokes of genius. The power of art over everything. Like the strength of water over stone, I apply a slow constant pressure.

We continued talking, cracking each other up, arguing, concluding each other's sentences. Three hours passed like seconds.

"God," she said, "you know it's funny, but I really feel like I can talk to you. Did I really just meet you?"

"I guess we fit together—"

"Because we're opposites . . ." she paused, thinking about everything that had been said, ". . . or because we're?—"

"Not," we said. We looked at each other for a moment, sensing something strange yet comfortable. . . .

I noticed her very delicate hands; uncoated nails; hands like Georgia O'Keefe's; I noticed scars on the inside of her wrists that resembled horizontal coke lines.

"The doctors said I killed all the nerves there."

I respectfully declined the invitation to pry. "I'd love to kiss them," I said, trying to read her mind.

She let out a nervous little laugh.

We discussed our love of tiger-boxer dogs, why animals were often more valuable than humans, how little dogs were a sign of fidelity and given as wedding presents—like the one given to the Arnolfino's at their wedding (my mother is a big believer in the healing powers of the fine arts and forced my siblings and I to take every course imaginable before we were 10, which is why I know all about that famous Jan Van Eyck painting of the Arnolfinos and am a big lover of Strauss; my father is more a believer in the sciences and math, he likes knowing the answer: that there is an answer, which is why my siblings and I had to take advanced and extracurricular subjects like macro biology). Julie and I didn't have an answer for why humans had waged conflicts in all but 14 years since our existence on the planet, or why landscapes were better than portraits of people like the Arnolfinos, except that maybe we are more animal than human, and nature is closer to purity than anything else.

"Let me finish showing you around."

She pointed out areas of interest on the 18-acre club—the fastest Deco II hard courts; the brick-red clays that ruined your socks; a breathtaking, open-air weight room, with gleaming silver free-weights, an Olympic-size pool, whirl pools, and Jacuzzis, all overlooking the murky green Atlantic, which rolled toward us on tiny curls of foam.

"I love the smell of the Atlantic!" she said, inhaling deeply.

"But not the Pacific," I said.

She looked at me as if she had received a small electrical shock. Her mouth opened slightly, for a second.

"Huh," she said, like OK.

She continued the tour, opened a door marked "READ-ING ROOM," revealing a grand British library—overstuffed leather arm chairs; dimpled, burgundy, leather "Chesterfield" couches; ceiling-to-floor bookcases; and oil paintings of fox-hunting scenes on forest-green walls. It looked like an English study, very *Masterpiece Theater*.

On the leather-topped desk sat a small, graceful bronze of a partially nude woman stomping a partially nude, bearded man: "Virtue Triumphing Over Vice" it read at the base. Both the male and the female were wearing togas that had become loose in the fight. One was wearing a wreath, the woman. Julie spun the large antique globe, showed me the gigantic dictionary, and pointed out the palatial white marble fireplace, with its green veins, containing black and white birch logs. . . . the fireplace was taller and wider than both of our bodies turned horizontal or vertical . . .

I picked up the phone and dialed: "Hi, Dad . . . I'm going to spend the night at Steve's. . . . Love you too, bye."

Leaning nude against the desk now, both of us bewildered and too tired to flip back over the couch, stayed put, hugging, motionless. Her arms draped around my neck, her head rested on my shoulder, then moved slightly, glancing at my numerous square red plastic wrappers on the Oriental rugs; we tossed our heads back and laughed, carefree.

"*God!*" she said.

"Who knew!" I said.

Her hair smelled like lavender and vanilla. I inhaled deeply as my fingers caressed the nape of her neck. I blew cool breezes around her neck. We were enjoying the warmth of the fire, basking in its glow, the mellow radiance of our bodies, and the way we fit perfectly with each other; to use her words, she slid her fingers along my abs, into all my "nooks and crannies." The smell of ocean salt whispered into the room through the windows, mixing with the aroma of the birch on fire. Her head nestled against my shoulder.

She whispered into my ear, "You won't want to see me again."

I chuckled, because that's what I do when I'm afraid.

She squeezed me very tightly, as if she were scared, and buried her head into my neck. I could barely hear the words: "I'm going pro." I felt a trickle of dampness on the side of my neck.

I looked past the French doors framed by green velvet drapes, out to an Atlantic, now glossy from the early evening sun. The sky was red and pink and orange, all brilliantly illuminated from behind by a fading sun that did not want to bow.

I tried to understand, put myself in her shoes. I lost all cares and sense of responsibility. I hugged her with all my strength. She reciprocated.

Time passed silently. The dramatic pastel sky faded to a chalky moon. She explained how her father 's father had always begun by rubbing the back of her dad's neck when he was a 6-year-old boy, then he would jokingly run his hands through the boy's large golden "David Copperfield curls," and then he would proceed to crawl his fingers up the 5-year-old's thigh while singing, "'The itsy bitsy spider . . .'"

No relative spoke of what they feared or confirmed. The boy, soon diagnosed as a mild epileptic, had looked angelic with his chubby cheeks and mop of sunshine curls streaming down. And this same boy became a father and sang the same song to her, not knowing why, but unable to stop, destroying the love she had wanted most.

Ostensibly, tennis-playing Barbie was still perfect for all who cared to look.

Her father could not acknowledge his shame. And he could not love what he could not comprehend. He mastered bourbon, squash, capital markets, epilepsy. But not her, not the defiant ram. Parent-teacher conferences, graduations, concealed humiliation, invisible hypocrisy, girls envious of her gifts, unvoiced shame….boys she would not let come close. The pistil removed from the flower. The flower that would not. Petals heavy with blood.

"He still thinks he's better than his father because he didn't do it to his son!" Her fist coiled. The bronze statue sailed through the air, slamming down on the worn Oriental rug. This was the fighter with the killer instinct that I had known.

Living in *"that house,"* she couldn't take it. She tried a variety of exit visas immediately after her reversal of fortune—numerous Neoflaxin, embracing a tree with a Porsche, "his Wilkinson double-edged razors."

So now, Juliet's wanting to become a prostitute would be what? So many unspeakable things: a way to disgrace the standard-bearer of a wealthy community, proof that love doesn't exist, something to do to fight ennui, false promise. I took her left arm from around my neck, kissed the little speed bumps on the inside of her wrist . . . heard the whisper of a moan.

For Halinka

POETRY

✽✽✽

POETRY

0…U.S. I

Screaming gusts of wind erupt off the Hudson
the hawk bites into my face with frigid fangs,
seizing my shuddering body
chilling me to the marrow

I claw my way up 8th Avenue,
clutching my coat like a man in a straightjacket
battling the lunacy known as New York winter

The tape rewinds
and the image quickly returns…

We're cruising down U.S. I in the Porsche
an ocean to my right, mountains to my left
my angel beside me

Tangerine hues flow
along the horizon line
guiding my mind to no place in particular…

Slowly
the sun acquiesces
to the moon's sumptuous luminescence,
a perfect pewter oval on indigo canvas

Time pauses to listen to Bird's flight
and standards of celestial beauty,
Set
just moments before
    fade,
and are eclipsed

Silence
is the dialectic of the canyon's haunting horn
Air
its stirring keyboard

Staccato
is the Pacific's rhythmic pounding
bass and percussion
entwining like lovers in the sand

Eros
Is
Is
Is Bird's anxious desire
His own love supreme
escaping like liquid dream
into warm night air

Into arms that want no more...

POETRY

I…JHVH @ 16

Why? Why do all the girls want to tutor him in French?
It makes me so mad — I hate myself for being jealous!
Their knees buckle when they glimpse him coming down
the hall, and they tell me why breathlessly

Because at 16 he has
Ebony eyes
Luscious mouth
seductive voice
winning smile
proven courage
nice hands
clean nails
slow touch
bow legs

A match

Nonchalance
Chinese eyes
chocolate skin w/
    cherry
          red
              under
                    tones

Maybe he'll let me speak
    on
         his
            MI-
                CRO-
                    PHONE

gladiator chest
perfect height
fly gear

wit
warmth
Nonchalance

        rap
            gift
                listening skills

He strolls by
smiles
says, "Hi"
They melt . . .
Even the gangsta babes have a gleam in their eye
and a bead on his butt

POETRY

2...Rose Petals: An Ode to Cun-nilingus

Earnest
love
this one true joy . . .

endless
laughter
rolling
as the seas

Ardor
speeds
moonlight's kiss

Slender shimmer . . .

afterglow . . .

eyes of bliss

Steaming—-
This one true power

MARK A. MILLS

Lilies perfume the dawn . . .

Tears of joy
kiss fragrant buds
and enter
Heaven's tower

POETRY

3... Nepthsis

Nepthsis

Your voice is like
the sound of
Eternity in the wind
hypnotic, mystical—
all around me

An angel's voice whispering
Love, love, love

On Nepthsis: Literally translated, her name means "head of the house." Revered as the head of the household of the pantheon, her protection was given to the matriarch of any household. She also provides bedside comfort to women in childbirth. Thought to be the mother of the guide of the underworld (Anubis), Nepthsis is often depicted riding in the funeral boat accompanying the dead into the Blessed Land, the heavenly afterlife of lush green fields. The sister of Osiris and Isis, and the wife of Set, she did not support Set in his bloodlust for power as he plotted to kill Osiris and usurp his throne. Rather, she aided her sister Isis in finding the pieces of Osiris's hacked body.

POETRY

4...Addicted

True arrows
Find open vistas
To the human heart leaving
Strangers thunder-struck
Lovers watching clocks
Anxious for 4:59—
The bolt to the elevator
That can't come quick enough
TGI—MFing—F
Means lost weekends in vertigo
Days pass seemingly in seconds
You tell me I make your body feel like wildfire
You rush to see me in your black sports car
speeding with the music deafening
When you arrive—
Your eyes are like a child's on Christmas morning
You tell me you don't know what's happening to you:
Your emotions are like wild horses
Running away

In between
heavenly gifts of bliss
I am celebrating like my all-time

Favorite team just won
The game of the century
I thought people
Only jumped up in the middle of Midtown Manhattan
screaming "Yes!"
in the movies
But here I am
Literally
Jumping
for joy
And frankly Scarlett…

Please! Please! Please!
Sunday nights finds me wanting to beg you not to go
But begging doesn't become me
So I grab you by the waist and pull you to my hips—
Demanding, "Where the hell do you think you're going!"
And it's on
again
Living la vida loca

POETRY

5...4 x 90 Degrees

Before the savanna and the slow
scalding sun
before nature that yields death
before epic struggles to rise and walk
before weighted chest and heavy eyes...

The summer's breeze off the sparkling sapphire Nile
its warmth between fingers as the sailboat glides
glittering like eternity's jewel

Not searching, but
coincidences entwined...

The essential as always
unseen...

Now
Melting horizon in front of me
the looming savanna
and beyond...
shifting mountainous dunes
Olympic heavens

The hourglass turns like the sun's burn...
slow
endless walking
shadows growing before my eyes
waves of memory
images of the tumult &
the shouting
Her
valleys,
pyramids of sand breaking under foot
sinking
sand-
paper throat
the ache of bones to the marrow's last photon
arctic desert night
mad wind without a home
soul amped by sorrow and doubt
screaming!

on the threshold of another world
doubled over
clutching my knees
as if holding on to my sanity and refusing to let go

Pink pastel sunrise
without a drop of dew
the mysterious radiance of the morning sand
its colors honey and blood
incandescent

no—
inflamed

The evidence of things unseen...
as always...essential

The Sahara's secret:
The sound of singing in daybreak's mass-like silence
angels?
the dead?
Elton John?

A shockingly vibrant tree on the desolate plain

The clear water cool & trembling, shimmering in the sun

The resilient bloom

in repose

born

Anu

POETRY

6...Hathor

You have no choice
you do not know why
When she comes through the door—
Brilliant
Purposeful
august
Radiance

You
are unknowingly
beaming

Her touch is
imperceptible

Petal soft

Yet
deeply
penetrating

Like laughing lovers
on a summer's day

Or a slow canoe
by the twilight's edge

POETRY

7...A Field of Poppies

Feathery kiss
Cartwheel twirl
A glow the sun's true nature
Clamped embrace
Upon this field of flowers

Wit, whimsy
a wink
Delights of life's Spring pleasures

Nimble mind, fine limbs like time
long and
without a care
A smile they caress

Neruda's song, so joyous now, laughter light as snow

To bask before such beauty grand
defies imagination

. . . so many colors in this Spring

      so many colors among these flowers

POETRY

8...New York @ Night

Merc S500:
Big black
luxury sedan
zooming down Park Avenue in Spring
its center islands of azaleas, lilacs, sunflowers
magic carpet cruise
more ship than car

Bright
scarlet carpet
Radiant
ruby door
Opening to
everyone
from everywhere
sculpted men
dazzling women
wit, charm, flirtation, discretion
civility

Sentences sparkle
Lines like
Smoke from incense
Smooth and just as fragrant

Music from Martinique
Marakesh
Mali
Rio
The Bronx
Blasts!

Complex,
this unifying queen Queen from Waset, sees me
hugs me joyously, giving freely the light within her—Supernova
kisses me
expressing nimble facility with XML Russian spitfire
Spanish
the strongest muscle's
greed
betrayals
deadly illusions—to be in love with love, the heart in Fall:
Autumn tears
A kaleidoscope of similar colors, lovers, none of which are
true

Purity
that dangerous reality—to risk everything for another, the
heart in Spring:
The color of ultimate friendship, an absolute, the willing-
ness for the ultimate sacrifice

The royal
Speaks with me about
Central European Jewry

I & I

British socialism
Red white and blue ethnocentrism

Her delicate sensibility
graceful intoxication
Her carefree melodic laughter
bliss
Ebony eyes glisten, penetrate
valiantly they try to x-ray, soothe, heal
Her soul sensing what she already knows
The color of the heart in Spring: regal black

POETRY

9...Isis

We dance with words
hustle samba freestyle
swaying
dusk till dawn
reggae blues rhythm
limbs sliding slipping
hips gyrating
backs arching
Furious drums
offering to the gods
enlightenment
Your braids flying
our world moving so quickly
Time jets
You whisper
imperatives and laughter
sweet as mangos
dripping with the knowledge
of a journey filled with
nectars
as delicious
as a sweet
love
song

POETRY

10...The Waves of Time

It is their first time:
This couple snorkeling
In Negril's
turquoise waters
They pause...and float
The water is warm and soothing
She is soft and nervous
Her hair is like spun gold, a sun-kissed mermaid
She adjusts carrots in her ear
as they bling sunbeams
She does not want to lose these presents from her lover
who is hard
confident
He presses his body to her bronze frame,
Kisses her tenderly, tasting the ocean's salt and her
slow tongue
Easing her fear's of the deep's mysteries
Vibrantly colored fish swim gracefully around their en-
twined bodies